CURFEW CHRONICLES

ALSO BY JENNIFER RAHIM

Fiction
Songster and Other Stories

Poetry
Mothers Are Not the Only Linguists
Between the Fence and the Forest
Approaching Sabbaths
Redemption Rain: Poems
Ground Level

Non-Fiction
As editor (with Barbara Lalla) *Beyond Borders: Cross Culturalism and the Caribbean Canon* (2009) and *Created in the West Indies: Caribbean Perspectives on V.S. Naipaul* (2011).

CURFEW CHRONICLES:
A FICTION

JENNIFER RAHIM

P E E P A L T R E E

First published in Great Britain in 2017
Peepal Tree Press Ltd
17 King's Avenue
Leeds LS6 1QS
England

ISBN13: 9781845233624

The author gratefully acknowledges the support of the
Toronto Arts Council in the writing of these stories.

CONTENTS

A NOTE ON BACKGROUND

On the 21st of August, 2011, the government of Trinidad and Tobago declared a state of emergency with an overnight curfew in response to a wave of killings associated with the escalation of organised criminal activity in the nation, including gang-related homicides, narcotics and human trafficking. Locations in Trinidad designated criminal "hot spots" were targeted. The exercise that was intended to last fifteen days was extended on September 4th and did not end until the 5th of December that year. The official opposition and social activists vigorously criticised the declaration of the extension – especially over enhanced police powers of search and arrest.

In its first five days, a quantity of guns and ammunition was confiscated, and over four hundred arrests were made, though many cases brought to court had to be dismissed for lack of evidence. There were accusations of racial profiling, and charges that the SoE (which undoubtedly had its supporters) was a distraction from Trinidad's deeply rooted problem of corruption, not only in the private sector, but also at the highest levels of the state. Above all, the widespread complaint was that the state's action targeted the "small fish" and that the elusive "sharks" behind them went unscathed.

But this is not the subject of this work of fiction, merely its background. *Curfew Chronicles* is an imaginative response to the undertones of those days. The book's concerns also extend to a broader reflection on some troubling aspects of the political and social climate of the post-independence nation state. The chronology of events is therefore not entirely literal. The tragic assassination of a prominent Trinidadian attorney (post-SoE), for instance, is woven into an interlocking narrative that navigates the porous border between fact and fiction. At the centre of this fiction are the private worlds and fortuitous encounters of a variety of Trinidadians that unfold during a day and night of that time.

... in all manner of things... all shall be well.

With deep thanks to

My parents, Bernard and Shirley-Ann Rahim, and all my siblings for their love; especially to Brent for his unwearied optimism; Anson Gonzalez for his contribution to poetry and generosity to the writers of Trinidad and Tobago, RIP; Earl Lovelace for his wonderful gift of story; Julie Marie Peters (SSM), Michael Stoeber and Nadine Ratiram for their support and appreciation of my journey and gifts; Barbara Lalla for her kindness; Jeremy Poynting for his patience with my process and for his dedication to writers' words; Dana Seetahal (SC), and in thanksgiving for her great light, RIP; all those who read some of these stories in their early stages, found merit in them and helped clarify details; and to the God of *All Good...*

SAVING WORD

The lady at No. 27 was always on time to catch the truck as it swung down Immortelle Drive. It was seldom late – seven o'clock every Monday, Wednesday and Friday morning. That was the routine. No real change.

She knew the truck. Someone had painted the words *Run Man* on the right side of the back loader. The driver was usually the same – close-trimmed pepper-grey beard and sunglasses, the lens rectangular shaped. He had mastered the art of reading his newspaper as the truck crawled, then surged along the street in response to the sharp "YEAH" from the two collectors.

Her ritual waiting at the gate offered a little window of wonder. The men's swift, purposeful movement buoyed her return to the sterile luxury of a house from which her children had all moved out. Their education began their exit. It was the life they had planned for them despite all those Independence parades, those hundreds of speeches about nationhood and service to country they had applauded, sitting among the other MPs. They had believed the ideals. Their life was on the island, but the children needed options. Let them see what the world had to offer. Home would always be there.

Her days were predictable. After the usual exchange of pleasantries with Ivan, the driver, and her husband's dash into the backseat of the Prado, with his brief, "Later", there were the orchids in the greenhouse to tend, Claudia to sort out with the day's chores, the short emails to the children, maybe a trip to the grocery, the mall or the hairdresser, lunch or tea with one of her old cronies from convent, or yoga – a recent interest. What had she done with her life, her gifts? What were they? Married to the Minister of All Things Legal – his new portfolio and hopefully his last. She wanted it all to end. She felt stained.

That morning, the black Prado did not just speed away. The heavily tinted window slid down. The Minister's arm, then face surfaced. She noticed the rakhi on his wrist, and seeing her glance, he withdrew his hand. That was why he was late last night. He had gone for prayers. He was uneasy about something, and needed again the faith he had, as far as she could tell, long relegated to necessary appearances at Pagwa and Divali.

Vague complaints about what he called the *challenges* of his office had dominated their conversations. She wasn't surprised at his choice of word. Governance here tipped too readily towards safeguarding the interests of one's side – and the dangled carrots of personal kickbacks. The business of the people weighed light. What wearied her most was what she suspected about the *means* employed to stay in the game, but those she was kept in the dark about – and maybe that was something of a twisted grace.

"The speech coming over at eight tonight. Live."

It was his way of saying that he wanted her to watch. He wanted, at least from that distance, to be sure of her support.

"Cook fish. I feel for shark."

Dinner was her charge that night. The trace of tenderness she had picked up in his request stirred an unsettling blend of gratitude and regret.

All the years – was that it, she wondered, as she considered his face.

"Fry it. Not too dry, okay?"

There it was again: the reproach, so slight that she always second-guessed herself. Did she hear it? Was it even his? He withdrew into the cabin too soon to see her nod. No matter. It was automatic. She was anticipating the arrival of the truck.

The men sprang into action as it broke the corner, one on each side, snatching bags and throwing them with precision into the cavity at the back. They vanished as quickly as they appeared, but she would try to see if she could recognize the collectors, to see if she could spot something about their individual behaviours that gave them away. She couldn't see their faces – they were often masked with bandanas or T-shirts tied Arab-style to protect themselves from the sun or maybe to filter the smell. Perhaps the masks were about something else. Mostly she noticed their practised sequence of actions, almost choreographed, so their work seemed to have the flow of a dance.

There was the one who liked to hop onto the back, using his single-handed hold of the grab-handle to allow his body to swing daringly sideways as the truck moved on. There was the tall, fit one who wore a red bandana tied gangster-style. He tucked his pants legs into knee-high socks. Those were more or less regulars. She knew them. Others came and went.

One night, at table, she had pondered aloud the possible reasons the men didn't stay long at the job. Apart from the two she recognized, the crew never seemed the same. The Minister did not raise his head. He was preoccupied with Claudia's Tuesday speciality of split peas rice and curry-stewed chicken, which he consumed in his habitual manner – chewing mechanically while he scanned the newspaper that was always neatly folded and placed on the side of his plate. She waited as though expecting at least an echo. Nothing returned but the sound of the newspaper being rearranged.

"It must be unpleasant work chasing after that truck all morning. No wonder they leave the job."

He surfaced from what seemed an immense distance, his eyes behind his reading glasses focused elsewhere, so she knew he was scrutinizing her every word as one would examine a glass for a crack.

At length he said, "Most of them are losers, Mavis. No

ambition. You see them." He wanted her to know he was aware of how she spent her mornings. The security man on the grounds reported directly to him.

She looked away feeling exposed.

"Such a shame – those waste-a-time-men. Costing the government millions. Those people are playing us well, and every government that gets elected. Like we owe them a living. People don't want to call it like it is. That is the problem."

He was baiting her. It was an old sore point – this feeling that he had liberated himself, a poor boy from Central, going to Naps and then law school in England. The last of eleven children brought up by a mother who couldn't read. He was a trailblazer, holding high government office, a man who had walked through whatever door he opened for himself. No one had done him any favours. Mavis recognized the trap, his way of provoking her so he could retell his creed: *Pull yourself up by your bootstraps*. She had decided long ago: *Girl, have nothing to say*.

That morning, when the truck appeared, Red Bandana was there, but not the other one. Something else was different, not with the men, but the truck. Someone had painted an over-sized *S*, maybe in protest, so that the sign now read, *RunS Man*. Catching the miracle, she smiled, buoyed by the saving word... Perhaps reading her reaction, Red Bandana waved and thumped his chest. She thought for a moment that he meant to say the work was his – he had made a noun of a command. The truck was gone when she discovered her hand poised to wave.

She walked towards the house feeling her world had suddenly grown larger.

WHAT THEY WANT

"Jus' give them what they want."

"Yuh not making sense, man. Things getting outta hand," Ragga protested.

The mere act of speaking drained him and, as though his weight was suddenly too much to bear, he sat down on the edge of the pavement, his face buried in his palms.

Keeper had cut off all his hair. Only his beard remained untouched. The block felt betrayed.

Ragga watched him jam his foot against the wall and lean back.

"Maybe we have the man wrong. Maybe he on another beat," Terence mused aloud.

He was perched on the wall that fenced the apartment block. The sun was at his back.

Keeper ignored the comment, aware that Terence was fishing for more and fanning Ragga's fire. He lit up and drew deeply on his cigarette.

"That poison going to kill you dead, dread," Ragga warned.

"I tried talk to the man," Terence put in.

Keeper exhaled slowly so that smoke veiled his face.

Ragga untied the bandana from around his neck and wiped the perspiration from his face. His work was done for the day, but he was uneasy.

"Look, this is twenty-eleven and we still in the same barrel. Hot Spot? What the hell is that? Crime living comfortable in big-shot house. The government blowing smoke in people eye."

Keeper laughed nervously and adjusted his propped leg.

"Everybody see my stylin'," Terence said, and lowered himself to the pavement to complete his point.

"Every two weeks I sit down by the barber. What we dealing with is a mind-set, Keeper. The move you claim to make telling them that they right – only bandit and drug-dealer living behind here."

"Tru' word!" Ragga exclaimed. "Let them know we have brains. Nobody grant them mandate to play people for fools. We doh 'fraid them. What they want – to cause riot on the place?"

"Look, this is no TV show where a man play hero and walk off free. Calm yuhself," Keeper urged. "We have to ride this one out. Stay low. Lawmen itching to look like they doing they wuk."

His cellphone beeped. He looked at the screen, then continued, "Ragga, yuhself bring the news about how the law rough up Prince down Monas."

"Yeah, they harass the wrong man. All them who-is-who they should be rounding up. But that doh happen in this place."

Ragga dragged the hat from his head and shook his locks free. They rested mid-back. He was tall, lean. A natural. His name was on account of the Carnival Saturday he'd danced until morning with a Jamaican woman who claimed Trini didn't have stamina. The fellas gave him the name after he had proved her wrong.

"Yes, I bring the news, Keeper. So don't tell me what I know already."

"I not saying we have to take stupidness," Keeper retorted. "Doh get me wrong. We jus' have to be careful. Lawmen looking to score points anyhow."

"But how you talking so, Keeper? " Ragga said. "Like yuh back against the wall. We cyah let *them* decide that is we who have this country in a mess. *Dat* kinda power I for one refuse point blank! Is a lie they giving the people, man. Yuh doh see?"

Keeper looked away, passed his hand over his newly shaven head.

Terence coughed and spat into the drain.

"That is not my band," Ragga continued. "If responsibility is what they want to dish out for all the wrong that going on, then everybody must take they fair share!"

He sprang to his feet as if ready for a fight.

"They want to look like angels by giving us this bogus devil mas' to play. Well, not me!"

"Look, you fellas don't have a parrot on a stick," Keeper said. "I have wife and my two girls to maintain. That is why I choose to give them whatever they want. They thirsty for criminals jus' to look good on the TV. So, I keeping low."

An uncomfortable silence fell. Keeper's rejoinder felt like a put down. They looked to him. It wasn't only his goalkeeping that had earned him the name he'd carried since school days. He was the man with ideas. They expected him to face the politicians when they came begging for votes. But he was getting tired of the role. With the girls now needing more, the pittance he got for off-loading containers for the storeowners around town wasn't enough. Maureen never complained, but he knew she wanted to do more than cashing chicken and chips.

Ragga broke the spell. He set off in a jog, south, towards Independence Square.

"Where the hell you going? Watch yuh back," Keeper shouted after him.

"Doh study me, pardner. Check yuhself."

"Well, since curfew have you lockdown, at least fix my radio."

Ragga lifted his hand to acknowledge that he had heard.

Keeper's phone rang again and this time he answered.

"Ok, doh worry. I going to pick up the girls."

Terence made like he was busy checking for messages on his cell. He could tell Maureen was on the other end of Keeper's call.

"What time they letting you off? Remind them is quite Port of Spain yuh have to travel."

Keeper pocketed the phone.

"Look man, I have to run. But keep an eye on Ragga. He too harden."

"Seen. He probably going Carenage to check for Prince. He not doing so good."

Keeper took a last pull and flicked his cigarette into the drain.

"You alright, Keeper?"

Terence's question was unexpected.

"Yeah man. Everybody stressed out. I no different."

"Ok, brother, but Ragga is no fool. And I not blind."

Terence walked north, as if to say Ragga could take care of his own stories.

"I too have eyes," Keeper muttered.

Just then a boy in a blue Superman T-shirt dashed by, looking over his shoulder as he ran, barely avoiding a collision.

"Watch it, youth-man!" Keeper warned.

The boy kept going. Keeper gave his watch a quick check. The cloth-people were expecting a container and would need fellas to offload. But there was time for another smoke.

That was one minute too long. Police jeeps appeared from nowhere. Gun. Baton. Fellas scampered all over the place like when ants nest raise. Keeper didn't even have time to run. The news went round like bushfire – he made the Twenty-One.

SCHOLAR'S LETTER

The talk reached Scholar that the government was planning to extend the SoE. The news came as he readied for the second leg of his daily routine since the curfew began – getting to the Promenade ahead of rush hour. First was his ten o'clock morning trip to Woodford Square. He made no stops on that trek. His lecture was at noon sharp, the lunchtime slot. That was his privilege as main speaker, but he always wanted to hear what others had to say. Listening to them gave him an opening.

The curfew had forced him to change his schedule. He ended his day at three o'clock, taking his time to push his reconditioned grocery cart east along Prince and south down Charlotte streets. He liked to follow the lawful stream of traffic, not like some of his comrades who barged their way in any direction they wanted. The law had its purpose – to keep justice in balance. That was his experience. Going with the flow gave him perspective. More than that – he saw when it was time to act.

Most of the vendors had grown accustomed to his daily passing and acknowledged him with a friendly nod. He wasn't a troublemaker, had never interrupted the earning of their bread. He enjoyed watching them arrange their goods, banter with neighbours, and haggle over prices with customers. He liked to see the people examining and re-examining their intended purchases – a pair of slippers, a jersey, a brassiere, a pound of tomatoes, a head of lettuce, provision – asking the usual questions, then buying or not, before hustling to catch a maxi or a bus.

He didn't like it when buyers gave in too quickly or allowed a vendor to make them buy what they didn't really want. There was no greater satisfaction than to hear people negotiate until a fair exchange had been made. The formula was simple.

Respect. Community. One education was needed in this place – for the people to know that power is theirs alone to bring to the table. Not the crab-in-barrel syndrome. Not the *What to do?* resignation. Or the panic to be a bogus kind of big.

He would include that in his next talk.

The natural current of the street always buoyed him, gave him courage to face the night and his thoughts. So he took his time, soaking in the sounds and smells of the city's life, the stream of bodies. All the small acts of living, like buying a hand of figs or refusing a sale, were decisions with futures attached to them. His business was to keep his daily appointment with the Square, telling it like it is, in and out of season. Thought – that was the real saviour for him.

At the end of Charlotte Street he paused to consider the Promenade. It was a gift to the city – *give Jack his jacket.* Scholar's policy was impartiality.

Drivers stopped for him to cross the street with the cart that contained all his earthly possessions. No matter how busy or crowded, there was enough time to allow a person to pass. It was good to hear, "Walk good, Pappy!" Or "Watch the traffic, Dads!" shouted from a driver. It was a small generosity that touched him.

When he got to the Promenade, he went east. His favourite bench was there, the one closest to the Cathedral and directly north of *The Focus* building. The intersection was a balancing point.

"Ole mas' all year 'round. That is the problem."

Scholar shook his head. His thoughts never let him rest, but the bench was a brief respite. He savoured the chance to sit there, just breezing, delighting in the city's changing moods towards shutdown. He watched, listened and felt, trying to regain his centre before he began his final leg past Columbus

Square, behind the Cathedral, to the shelter adjacent to the William Scott building – a parking lot with space allotted for the homeless. Somebody's bright idea that motor cars and street-dwellers were somehow interchangeable.

A few smartmen had tried to cash in by renting prime spots to newcomers and general walkovers. This didn't go well with Scholar. He had no taste for petty territorial politics, preferring to be at his ease in the open square and, when it rained, under a suitable building. The curfew, though, had made finding a decent corner to bed down for the night a new necessity. Nobody wanted to risk arrest, so space was in high demand in the shelter.

The news that the SoE might be extended was a disappointment. He heaved himself off his bench and got going again. The ple-plonk, ple-plonk of the cart's damaged wheel and the racket from the metal frame kept up a discordant mantra with his musing: *SoE extend. More SoE. SoE extend. More SoE.* The acronym had the perfect tragic meter, like a flame leaping and falling and leaping again as it resisted its inevitable end. The renewed emergency, he felt, fell in line with the general bacchanal.

He came to a halt at silent Columbus.

"SoE, indeed!"

His analysis of the state of the nation had won the approval of the audience at his lecture that day. It pleased him to end the work-week on a high note. The speech was his best ever. He had ended with a metaphor that would make those hotshot writers look small. "This Sunday," he'd said, pausing for effect, "make it 14 days we chipping down with this band they name *De War on Crime*. Well, when the music stop, what next? *SoE Part II?* My fellow citizens, let me offer you an educated guess..." He paused again, relishing the anticipation he sensed in his regular listeners, waiting until he felt he had fully drawn them in to drop his ace: "There will be Part II alright – only the colour on the ballot paper will be different."

The applause was spontaneous, though the trademark

ambiguity of his closers never sunk in immediately. That delay was always carefully orchestrated. It was his gift – to fire their minds with the need and possibility of change. The rest was reserved for the post-speech debate. The *What the hell yuh really saying* part that enlivened the square's discussions.

Everyone cheered, even his most fervent opponents like Preacher, who felt that the SoE was a sign that we were finally on the road to change. Things had to get bad before better could come. Diehards from the opposition camp took that to mean the New Sun government would fall. Too damn corrupt! They give *tief* a new meaning. There was the Anybody-Who-Feel-They-Could-Do-Better section that followed Maverick. They boasted of having no allegiance to any party and wanted to know if Scholar wasn't happy that the SoE was cleaning up the city, making it safe to walk town without worry about which bandit was going to rob him of the nothing he owned in his rickety cart.

Nothing fazed Scholar. He possessed such clarity in the fray of debate it was hard to believe he was the madman people called him.

"It is the prerogative of the free to have opinions." And without a trace of ill-will he added, "For those with eyes to see and ears to hear, the reality is that the criminals in this land, wherever they are located, in or out of those so-called Hot Spots, have been given higher level approval by this shameless hoax to take a holiday. You know what I mean – a little R&R in Tobago while the authorities busy themselves collecting dysfunctional and obsolete weaponry. What we are witnessing, my friends, is a far cry from serious politics!"

More than anything, Scholar prided himself on being a professional. He would not be dragged into a brawl. There were standards to maintain.

"We have been hoodwinked. You understand? Ganja and outdated artillery are not evidence of what is real. I am saying, whatever the colour of your jersey, this country needs a new day. This whole place should wear white for a change. There is nothing inherently wrong with that non-colour – and it is not a recommendation to join any party with that motif. I am simply saying we have to rethink how we want to engage this thing we call INDEPENDENCE."

He left them holding that think-card until his next session. People depended on him to push the borders, even if that meant disagreeing with him. He took that responsibility seriously. It had earned him his name. The SoE was turning out to be more than a brief inconvenience; it stirred in him a greater sense of urgency. He had to reach a larger audience. The situation was grave.

"A state of comess!" he announced to no one in particular, and made an about turn and headed back to the Promenade and his bench.

From his cart he took a blank piece of cardboard and, with the half pencil that was forever lodged behind his ear, began to write a letter to the editor. The delay would mean losing a good spot at the shelter, but what did that matter? He had to act.

The words came quickly, as if they were awaiting his hand, so the final full stop wasn't far behind. He retrieved the necktie he had removed after his lecture. He never spoke without it – a schooldays' habit. Trusting in the good faith of the city, he left his cart unattended and made the crossing to *The Focus*, certain of a successful outcome. Smithy, his old school pal, used to be the big chief there. He had never once passed Scholar's station at the Square without stopping to say hello and exchange a few ideas. So, although there was a new man in charge, Scholar was confident he would get a decent hearing.

A SALE

The land couldn't find a new owner. That was no secret. More than three years on the market and nothing. Only bush and more bush occupying the lot. People came from all over the place to see it. Some of them treated the trip like an outing, packing their vehicles with coolers and food so that they could stop by a few beaches on the way to take a dip in the sea and relax with friends and family. The agent, Mr. Craig, Lucky to the locals, was always on spot to meet them. He dealt patiently with a whole set of questions about the square-footage, the deed, the soil, the wind, the runoff from the rain, the MP for the district, the regularity of the water supply, the damage caused by sea blast, the dependability of the bus service to Grande, who in the area was a good builder and – what about crime?

Lucky responded generously, even struggling to climb the hill to the back of the property with them, clearing a path with his cutlass to show the view from that elevation, pointing out the Tobago coastline and politely rebutting their suggestions that what they were seeing might be Venezuela. He would get them to imagine the map of the island and clarify their present location, until finally everybody agreed, yes, that there was Tobago.

"A man could swim that distance easy-easy, if he had the mind," he added, trying to evoke for them the daredevil bushman he felt they expected to find in the place. Nobody ever took him on.

They came and left, giving the assurance that they would think about it, promising to call the next day but, in the same breath, asked whether there were other properties in the area for sale. He played along with them, but expected nothing.

The problem was that the western end of the property bordered a cemetery. Not even the village children ventured to pick the huge guavas from the tree that grew on its boundary, standing there on the threshold between worlds. Everything was perfect about the place but that. So they were not convinced by his glib reassurance: *Is the living yuh have to 'fraid, not the dead.* An awkward silence would descend – the signal of the goodbyes to follow.

"Yes man, you know how to find me. I not going nowhere," he would say, sounding upbeat. What he really meant was *The land wasn't going anywhere.* But that wasn't good business.

In truth, he never felt any real disappointment at the failure to make a sale. The greater value was the chance to make another trip up the coast to show the property. He would make a day of it, leaving Arima early and taking his time, stopping in Valencia by the doubles vendor and standing by the roadside so that people could see him. Somebody he knew was sure to hail him out. Balancing the hot doubles in the palm of one hand, he would lift the other to return the greeting. At Matura, Rampanalgas and Cumana, he did the same thing. Making stations: stopping to buy a packet of cigarettes, salt biscuits, power mints, a cold beer or a sweet drink.

Each village was a chance to breathe the air, watch the life, talk with an acquaintance or some pumpkin-vine relation. His need for connection intensified especially when he drove through the shady patches in the road where the forest made a canopy, or the places where the sea peeped through the trees. The place he had abandoned was the very place that was calling him back. The problem was he didn't want to answer.

Now this big-name lady from way down townside was interested in the land.

"So you have people from up here?"

Lucky looked at her from the corner of his eye. Not from any motive to be sly, but he knew his guess was right.

"Not from here, no."

Her tone was brisk and frank.

"A lady like you want to live in this far place? It could be lonely – all by yuhself out here."

"You are making assumptions, Mr. Gentleman."

She looked him straight in the eye.

He got the message. It buoyed him that she lived up to his expectations. No foolishness. Brave – just like in the newspapers. He didn't feel the need to let on that he knew who she was. After all, she called no attention to that part of herself. He liked that. No highfalutin nonsense. But he could not put his finger on the uneasiness he felt about her need to be this far away.

"So yuh sure about the spot?"

"It's perfect. Exactly what I'm looking for."

"See that hill over there? It will block out the light. This place far from town. Plenty driving... Yuh could handle distance?"

He watched her carefully as she surveyed the plot, her eyes beaming satisfaction.

"This is what I want, Mr..."

"Craig is the name."

"Yes. Sorry."

"Craig," he said again.

The first viewing and she wanted to close the deal. No friend or family on the coast to stand with her, but she wanted to build. It didn't make sense. He heard himself highlighting realities she should weigh more carefully: the sea blast, the damp from the closeness of the mountain, the need for a drain and retaining wall that would drive up building costs. He tried to keep a neutral, professional tone, but felt a stirring like anger at her certitude – or ignorance or stupidity. It didn't matter which; he only knew that he didn't want to close the sale. She was suddenly the possibility that he would lose his one reason to drive up the coast. It was time to drop his trump.

"Yuh know, Miss, that is a cemetery over there."

"Oh, yes? Where?"

She held herself on tiptoe. She was short. He pointed to the far end of the property, side-glancing the lady, waiting for the anticipated reaction. People were always turned off by that detail.

"Jus' behind those trees. Hard to see from here. Too much bush."

"Really?"

Curiosity. That is what he heard. The information intrigued her. She stepped further into the overgrowth, then stopped to get her bearings and peered ahead, wanting to confirm for herself what he had said. Seeing nothing, no mounds of earth or headstones to prove his claim, she turned to meet his gaze with a question on her face.

"Is it still in use?"

"Nah, not again. The burial ground move to up by Mission. Landslide – no more access road."

The cemetery was the turning point in every showing, yet the town-lady continued to pick her way through the razor grass, black sage and ti-marie, heading in the direction of the guava tree. The ripe fruit were soft bulbs in the late afternoon sun.

"People say the dead like to congregate by guava tree."

"I thought jumbie preferred cotton trees."

"True, but plenty people say guava is the scent that call the dead to cross over. "

"Interesting."

She pressed on. He watched her determined advance, allowing a reasonable distance to open between them, letting her have her adventure, before following at a more leisurely pace. Even with his damaged calf, his height and tall-tops gave him an advantage she didn't have, but didn't seem to care about, even in her trendy lawyer's suit. What puzzled him most was her need for distance. Something was at the other end of the road she had travelled. The trouble that was brewing with her investigations – a homicide with possible links to a high-level narcotic ring was all over the newspapers. Kingpins could topple. Was that it? Or maybe she was seeking to give a bigger welcome to the place, allow it to make her more its own. A knot tightened in his throat. He needed a diversion.

"Some people say the land here possess."

"With what," she asked, and reached up to grab a full, ripe guava.

She sank her teeth into its flesh. Her indifference ruffled him.

"I not joking, Miss," he said. "Dead people bury over there. I only telling you so you would know the property you want to buy."

"Really? Maybe that's why the guavas are so big. All that good manure!"

She gave an impish smile and took another bite.

He watched, suspended in admiration at her display of ease. She was already at home. He reached up to pluck another guava and handed it to her.

"One for the road."

"Fuh sure," she said, welcoming the gift with a quick whiff.

He waited until she was strapped in, aware of his struggle to surrender to the prospect that she had found what she was looking for. That can happen. Maybe her spirit took to the place. He listened to the smooth, efficient turn of the engine.

"I'll be in contact with the agency, Mr. Craig. I'd want to settle the sale as soon as possible, ok."

"Everything in order, Miss. You have my word."

"Nice. By the way, what is the name they call you up here?"

"What yuh mean?"

"You know… other than Craig."

That touched him, her wanting to know more of himself than he had shown.

"Lucky. That is what they call me."

"Thanks. Take care. You will hear from me tomorrow, Mr. Lucky."

The car moved off, slowly, like a thought completing itself.

"Yes, lawyer-lady. Yes. Tomorrow will see for itself."

The insistent throb of his wounded leg won his attention. The clear blue of the late afternoon sky showed no sign of rain. He had come to associate different intensities and qualities of pain with various natural phenomena or premonitions.

"Hmmm..." he muttered and drove off with the scent of guava trailing behind.

HAIR

People say the whole of Carenage hear Prince bawl when soldiers hold him down and cut off his locks. He bawl so loud, the sound travel across the sea from Gasparee and wake up the prisoners on Carrera. It travel until it make landfall, like the mournful echo of a far cry. It had people wondering what douen was trying to get a hearing, or if it was a warning that somebody was going to meet with death. Talk say a fella in a pirogue bringing contraband from Venezuela hear Prince bawl and get so frighten he dump all the goods he was carrying in the sea. That same fella end up dead in Claxton Bay the next day because he pull ashore empty.

And this could jus' be plain idle talk, but a Baptist woman fresh from mourning ground give a witness that when she was walking on the shores of Guinea, somebody bawl out from the other side of the ocean, and that was about the exact time the soldiers were doing their wickedness on Prince head. And if that is 'nancy story, the very next day, a well-known sadhu from Carapichaima told his followers that he'd had a dream – somebody shave his head clean, and the moon wasn't even new. Not at all a good sign.

Anyway, since then, Prince stop talking. Not a word. He not eating either, like he sorrowing but he can't name the pain. Whole day he sit down on the beach drawing something on the sand that people decide must be Africa because it take that shape, and Prince is a conscious man. But not everybody agree. Some say it look like a chicken breast. The man must be hungry. But that is dotish talk looking for company. Prince doh touch meat. They wonder if it could be India, because of how it narrow down to the end. Talk didn't stop there. Somebody claim it was the whole damn world he was drawing – flat out – so nothing missing and everybody represent. And in truth, Prince was that kinda fella. Human being is human being – one Father.

Who is to say what the man was doing? People like to run they mouth, so reasons never in short supply. Prince not talking, only shaping and reshaping his map that had no name – except that, depending on who doing the looking, it shape like what they say. The new talk is that Elder diagnose the situation – is travel he travelling. Harry, who was Prince half-brother on his father side, agree with that one.

"Is a serious, serious thing. Yuh jus' cyah come outta the blue and mess with a man head. That is sacred. People doh have respect again!"

The man wasn't breaking no law. Harry was the one who convince Prince to go Gasparee to lime by a pardner, Dean, and kill some time with all this curfew business going on and nothing much doing. The hardware was slow and nobody want transport for goods, so the truck park up. Prince wasn't in the thing at first, but las' minute he ups and say he going. Harry and them fellas throwing down a few drinks and playing card, but Prince upstairs sleeping dead when trouble come. They say they looking for ammunition and drugs. Now if you know Dean, he is a man that like his rum. And is true his fingers a little sticky. But guns and drugs – that is another business. The problem is nobody ask nobody a proper question. But good licks share.

The whole episode end-up in the papers with Harry holding up Prince locks for the camera. The mystery is what he *didn't* tell the reporter. Although he was careful to gather up every strand and put them safe to one side – because Prince would want that – is only two he could find to show the camera. The rest just ups and disappear.

Disappear? People like story. The latest is that Prince

missing hair reach quite to Port of Spain in the people Parliament. How it land there? That was the question. The cleaner-lady make the discovery – Prince locks sit down comfortable in the Speaker's chair like it had something important to say. At first she figure somebody was making bad joke. So to keep ole talk from making young, the best thing was to remove the evidence to save any undue interruption to the serious business of the House. But then it struck her what was really going on. The object on the chair belong to Prince – she being a second cousin to the man and know him well. That is how the story leak out.

That news had the place wondering what the france the rest of Prince hair was doing out there. But that is to tell you how people believe anything for a story.

A FISH TALE

Miss, yuh shoulda be there / to see dem Big Fish dance / like dey have no worries. / Friday an' we dodging de guard / 'cause to tell de honest truth / Sherriff boat not authorize / and SoE harassing everybody. / Is honest living we making, Miss, / and life hard – / even fish in lockdown. / I have eyes. / Racket like peas on de sea / and PO-lice too / have to eat ah food. / But Miss, ocean have plenty road, / and we stay clear of de avenue dem bandit travel on. / Nothing blind my eye. / Moon full / and dem Big Fish / happy as pappy, / playing deyself, / drinking Johnny Blue, smoking Cuba, / and yes, / walking on water too. / Dat is what I see. / Sheriff and Illegal, / dey was with me, / but dem doh believe. / Nothing biting and time boring / so they relax / and sleep fall, / BRAPS! / Not me. / Sea is no bed for human being. / And Miss, / Dem Big Fish dance! / Smiling currency. / Things nice. / De Law only catching small-fry. / I not bragging / but I too have a t'eory / though I never go no UWee. / I giving you one little hint: / how Jesus walk on water / have nothing to do with how dem Big Fish gallery / like dey hit a vincy. / Trus' me.

The whole story came back to Gladys word for word, like a poem she had memorized. That was how he had spoken it, and she had listened, mesmerized by his tale. Now he was standing at the side of the road, flagging her down, in fact any car that was heading his way. She stopped because she remembered his story. In his white T-shirt and jeans, he cut a different figure from their encounter at the fishing depot. That time he was barebacked and wore only a pair of black shorts that glistened like fish skin. He'd noticed that she had brought no bags and volunteered to guide her to the little shop where she could buy at a dollar each. That was when he told his story – his response to her asking how the fishing was going. At the end, she laughed and said he could tell a good tall tale. She remembered his parting rejoinder.

"Miss, I look like I go lie to a nice lady like you?"

"And what if I not so nice?"

He smiled at her comeback and volunteered to take her purchases to the car. She was struck by his stocky limbs, his short stature.

"Drive safe, Miss. The road doh eat nice up here."

He held her gaze, confident in his knowledge of the place.

"I make yuh out from the papers, yuh know," he said. "Seetal, correct?"

He didn't need confirmation.

Now he was peering at her through the passenger window.

"So yuh make meh out? I going townside."

"Ok. Jump in," she responded.

He gestured to the sizable cooler he held.

"Pop the trunk, thanks. Is fish I have in here."

He was back in a flash.

"We good to go."

He drew the seatbelt across his chest and clamped it shut. He smelt of bath soap and cologne.

"Thanks for the ride. A family having a thanksgiving tomorrow and they want me to make broth."

Pride glowed in his smile.

"Yuh does eat shark? One is yours if yuh want."

"But you asking answers, man. "

That delighted him. He settled back into his seat and she noticed that his feet barely touched the floor. He wore black suede ankle boots, visibly worn. She saw that the back of the right side was mashed in.

Somewhere along the winding road down through Cumana to Matura, she learnt that his name was Hubert Constantine.

"This coast is home."

They exchanged glances. It was not simply information. He talked a mile a minute about everything under the sun – the state of the nation, politics on the coast, problems with the roads, his admiration for Obama, his family in Florida. He didn't seem to need a response, but she noted that he revealed little about himself. Next the talk turned to her. He had heard she was buying land on the coast and was going to build.

She said nothing, taken aback at how quickly the word had spread. Perhaps he was just speculating, trying to pick her mouth.

"I could do masonry, yuh know. That is my trade."

Her glance must have communicated doubt. He quickly added, "Ask anybody. But the sea – *dat* is a love."

He had become, in that instant, so much himself that she could not look away.

"Watch de road!" he warned. "Fellas here drive like they have early appointment with St Peter."

A quick adjustment of the steering wheel righted the vehicle.

"Things get real tie-up out there these days."

He looked towards the ocean.

"The owner giving the boat a rest until this SoE business cool down. Peter paying for Paul – and that doh mean wrong-doings not going on… That out there is the sea."

She noticed that his last sentences came unevenly, suggesting self-censure or a need to be defensive, although she had offered him no challenge. Maybe he had remembered his fish story and what he'd disclosed about the boat he worked on not being registered.

"Anyway, in case yuh looking for a mason, check me out. I go fix you up like family. Yuh go like yuhself when I done."

He leaned forward, pulling up the pant leg to his knee,

obviously feeling some discomfort. She glimpsed the undressed wound on the back heel.

She involuntarily sucked in air and asked, "How did that happen?"

"Sardine tin," he replied dismissively and lifted the foot so that she could better see his wound was fresh.

"A bad habit I have."

Her look told him he needed to explain.

"I doh like wearing shoes."

He grinned sheepishly.

"Shoes, that is what they call me," he added.

"Interesting," she replied and left it there.

The drive continued without much conversation after that. She didn't mind. It was enough to look at the changing shades of green quickened by light and breeze. It was enough to see the quiet content of faces as she passed by small villages, and the patient rooting in tomorrows of houses built in increments. That life reassured her, confirmed her commitment to the fight she could not surrender, and allowed her to put down for a while what most troubled her.

For the first time in her life, she felt that the place was losing ground, slipping away to where not even justice could throw a saving rope. That was the real emergency – some hydra of greed that needed, above all else, to be rescued from itself. Otherwise the entire nation would be held hostage to lies – the very law, for that matter. More than the death threats, that distortion terrified her, and she felt the need for space. Not to run away, but to find the strength for the battle ahead. She needed the chance to wake up to a new horizon. The coast offered her a place to visit with beginnings each morning.

The stone pillars planted on either side of the road to mark Valencia's boundary came into sight. Shoes made an unexpected request.

"You could put me down here. Thanks."

Gladys pulled to the side of the road, holding at bay her

curiosity about his change of plan. He had said he was headed to Port of Spain.

"Now don't forget to pop the trunk," he said casually.

His exit was brisk in spite of his wounded heel. In no time his face was at the window on the driver's side.

"Now, have a blessed and productive rest of your day."

He was gone before she could say goodbye.

Her final glance saw him scurrying across the road with the cooler propped up on his shoulder. His target was a bar that was celebrating its recent makeover with a sale on beer. A man lingered in its shade, a Stag bottle hung in his hand.

"Walk good, Mr. Constantine." She addressed the mirror, suddenly aware that the story of his alias was his way of letting her know a small truth – that he was more than his name.

DUMB-STRUCK

In the middle of the prayer session – jus' so – Sumintra couldn't open her mouth. The team handpicked by Pastor for the ministry of intercession was gathered to pray for the nation. Her lips were in lockdown. Unbelievable. The chief prayer couldn't make a sound. A battle royal was at hand. The nation was in crisis. From captain to cook were in need of salvation. Too much damn corruption. The place had sunk to its lowest low – fleas in the White House, the wanton thievery of public funds, ministers in international sporting scandals, private churches constructed with the people's taxes, a prophetess on the run, illegal highways mashing up the mangroves, weedlike substances in a top official's house, boobs-grabbing on a flight from Tobago. The list was long. *Gone to the dogs*, in the words of an esteemed senior counsel.

The prayer meeting was in full swing – everyone united to storm heaven. With the praise and worship finished, the Prophets almost at the end of sharing whatever word or vision had come, the Intercessors readied themselves to do their thing. Eyes and ears were focused on Sumintra – Sister Judith to the church. She was their leading prayer. Words flowed from her like a flood, and always artfully strung with the proper quotes from the Good Book and with key lines from Pastor's Sunday sermons. She paid attention and wrote notes in a copybook during every sermon. She knew just when to lift or lower her voice, when to pause – and when to lose all words so that only the loud clack of tongue against palate, or the breathless "Aaah yes Lord" could come. No question, Sister

Judith was a mighty intercessor. Serious about her salvation – that is what the church knew about her. The group depended on her to start and close every session.

But when the time came for Sister Judith to pray, nothing came. Not a sound. Those who had their eyes closed opened them; those who could not see her, shifted to catch sight of the sister. Pastor was there. Not his usual practice, but the circumstances were urgent and the flock needed his presence. The women considered it an honour and wanted to assure him that they were fruitful prayers at their stations. Time came and the sister's mouth would not open.

The members felt a flush of panic, but no one had the courage to step forward. Pastor coughed and flipped the pages of his Bible, seeking a word to bridge the gap, to get the members in gear and comfortable. Nothing. The sister's lips were sealed shut. Pastor coughed again. An intervention was necessary. He slapped the book shut so vigorously the hall thundered. Everybody looked up. Not Sumintra – she hit the ground, put down by an invisible hand. Not since that time way back, when she had made her way to the Mercy Seat, had that happened.

Pastor began to speak.

"Church, the Lord says... Yes, indeed He says to his people, this blessed day, Galatians 6:9, take note of it: *Let us not be weary in well doing: for in due season we shall reap, if we faint not.* Amen?"

"Amen," the prayers chorused.

"Today, church, we will not grow faint. Oh no, heaven forbid!"

Taking that to mean the sister should be helped back to her feet, a few willing hands moved forward, but Pastor raised his hand.

"Leave her. Let the Good Lord do His work. Search your hearts... search them so you may not be found wanting."

All eyes found the fallen member. The word had to be for her. They had not been found wanting.

"Comprehensively slain."

That was the verdict. A fresh spirit of fervour moved through the gathering. It was time to pray.

There was one thing Sumintra had long ago accepted. Nobody had put a gun to her head and sent her that day to the offices of Housing and Settlement to beg – no to plead, play martyr, whore, whatever – so that somebody would agree to expedite her case for a house. Twenty years to wait for a set of keys was not right. Plenty people were in the same boat, waiting and waiting for a miracle that would push their names to the top of the list. All manner of pull-string and curry-favour was taking place with officials fixing things up for friends and family. Something had to be wrong with that.

No. She wasn't a girl just from school, so she couldn't claim that big man with position advantage her, so people could feel sorry for her. That was not the case. The decision to place herself at the disposal of the Minister was hers alone. Nobody sent her that morning, freshly showered, six-inch stilettos and smelling of imitation *Obsession*. Her mind was set on one thing: a house, a space of her own. Her formula was simple. Give him a piece of the action like talk said was his way. She had read the papers, the reports of alleged indiscretions. She wouldn't be the first to work the system.

So when the terms were put to her that morning, she had considered herself neither martyr nor whore. Let the self-righteous satisfy their need to play clean. Her mission was clear. No, there was no one to blame. She had come prepared, but in the middle of delivering the Minister's "small favour" the scheme began to come apart. She was pulled to depths she had no desire to revisit – the day she found her father in that dingy room smelling of insecticide, the sight of his naked backside, and Miss Lutchman pressed to the wall of her shop, moaning in a way that wasn't at all about pain. What to make of that?

That connection broke her. Walking away, trying to hold her back straight, she knew she had lost the game. Her insides heaved and their contents joined the mess of the city, trickling away in a drain on South Quay. In her head was the father she had supposedly taken after, with no brains, no ambition to do more than his gardening and market selling. Not enough for her mother who wanted so much more from him. Sumintra was a reminder of that disappointment.

"Well at least you could count."

The taunt was aimed at her cashiering and bagging groceries for a pittance at Ali's mini-mart.

"The man can't give change, after all them years selling market. My eye have to be in he tail. Cyah count to save he life!"

During those outbursts, her father never defended himself. Did nothing but drop his leg from the hammock and kick-off to put it in motion. Said nothing, his only reply the croak of the ropes and the hum of his favourite bhajan. Maybe that was the truest response he could make for his life outside the house, beyond the garden he planted, and the botched sales he was accused of making on market days. They couldn't have cost them much. Even if he could not count, they never wanted for anything.

Silence was his means to save his other life, the one Sumintra had stumbled upon at *Lutchman's Garden Supplies*. She didn't like the shop, but she liked going out with her father. He took her into rumshops where she sat on high barstools and watched him fire back shots in raucous conversation with his friends. He bought her perilously orange corn curls and ice cream in little cups that she ate with sweet-smelling wooden spoons – all their secret. It was the reason he winked at her when his wife launched into the lectures directed at her for always coming close to last in every school test, while her siblings were their teachers' pets. Her mother's creed: doctor, lawyer, and if you couldn't do better, teacher – always in that order.

"Dat chile head hard," she complained to her unresponsive husband. Then came her unfailing anthem. "Is you she take after, Boyie. Not Vishnu, not Rajindra, not Leela. Them have brains. But she…"

In the middle of the Minister's favour, she remembered again why the father she loved never cared to defend himself against the insults or complaints. She had never really thought about what happened during those outings to buy seeds, but she knew that when she agreed to the terms that would guarantee her a house, she had betrayed Miss Lutchman – who couldn't even see that she deserved better than that toxic back room, or having to stand like a shadow on the edge of the mourners at her father's funeral.

Sister Judith's mouth couldn't open. Not a word. All the *Lord, have mercy, Lord,* she had uttered to wash herself from the stupidity that proved her mother right. All the *Lord, Lord* she had cried, the hours of churchgoing and praying for sinners to find the salvation she had found. All the *Lord, Lord* that made her feel she was something in this world, like Leela and the rest of them now in foreign, with houses that had basements and offices with their names and titles on the doors. At least she was something they could not claim to be – *saved.* All those years of praying, but secretly not wanting the same *Lord* she carried around like a trophy to be also theirs. Praying Sunday after Sunday for a nation that was on the road to perdition, but loving more the advantage that they, the chosen, believed they had – as though they had a monopoly on virtue, and God. Praying long prayers for all those people, and for what – a salvation she couldn't grant her own self?

All the strength in her legs was gone. She smelt, once more, the foul air of the agri-shop, saw her father's naked backside and felt anger, never confronted, make a knot her throat. She heard anew her mother's pain and Miss Lutchman's stifled pleasure; she saw them together, for the first time, her mother and the other woman, with her father in the background, rocking contently in his hammock. She had never seen their suffering as her own.

Once again, she was on the pavement in Port of Spain, with people hustling to get where they were going. Just so, the contents of her belly were on the floor of the meeting hall. When the intercessions stopped, and with Pastor's hand pressing down a little too heavily on her head, praying for fetters to break, she knew it was time to put an end to her mourning, to close the chapter on the long sentence of atonement she had given herself.

She rose from her faint with the sisters rubbing her back and telling her, "No need to feel bad, dearie. It could happen to anybody. Mercy is the Lord's."

Sumintra had one mission in mind. She was going to face the Minister. It was time to come down from her cross.

STORM

When the Promenade saw the security throw Scholar from *The Focus* like a bag of rubbish, it was sure that was the cause of the storm. It lashed Port of Spain hard, then spread out to every corner of the island, even Tobago. Met Office officials in Piarco didn't know what to say; none of their instruments could explain; they hadn't seen it coming. No logic could account for the rains that dowsed the island like a cleansing. But the Promenade witnessed the exact moment when the first raindrop struck the pavement. It had a front seat view on the happening: Scholar. They had no reason to treat the man like a criminal. No right to disrespect the fella – madman or not. So the complaint went. Town was vexed.

Poor Amber. She was at her station in the reception hall when Scholar came through the door. Up to that point, the day had passed without incident. In between the usual watching and waiting, she had found the time to jot a few lines in her notebook. The job demanded little of her; to compensate, she wrote to stave-off the feeling that she was marking time. The piece that came in spurts as the day dragged on looked promising, a good addition to the collection she was forever putting together. Calvin called them her *Dear Marion, poetries*; told her they wouldn't pay her bills. He always claimed to be joking; she pretended indifference.

Jus' so, with only minutes to closing, the day took a turn for the worse. Scholar entered the building, a piece of cardboard pressed to his chest, and asked to see the editor *forthwith*. She was in for a challenge and didn't want to mess up. Whatever the drawbacks, working security at *The Focus* was a convenient detail. Nice environment. Close to home. Newspapers to read when things were slow. Plenty time for her jottings. The city right outside the door. She could take lunchtime walks in search of inspiration. But now here was this madman looking like he wanted to cause trouble.

Scholar had dressed for the anticipated meeting. He was decked in his Sunday best, an oversized grey jacket (in need of laundering), trousers secured with a length of electrical cord and a used-to-be white shirt finished with a black necktie. *The Focus*, he felt, had no rival as the carrier of his letter to the nation. Smithy had given the paper character and depth. His track record was incomparable. He had been committed to the people's business. He had bequeathed a legacy. A path to follow.

Amber sized up the situation. What to do? Her training came back like rote. Rules of engagement: *At all times communicate respect but strength.*

"Sir, you have an appointment?"

"Appointment. I don't need one, Miss. My colleague was the late Mr..."

She didn't wait for him to finish.

"Mr. Who? Look, you can't see anybody now. We closing jus' now. So please leave the premises."

She wanted to send him packing before Cummings and Randolph returned from their rounds.

"Young lady, you do not understand. I have an urgent letter." He drew attention to the piece of cardboard. "This," he said, "must go to press. The nation needs the benefit of my opinion."

The man had gone too far – full of himself. There was a word for that. *Arrogance. Narcissism.* She toyed with the possibilities.

"Miss, my insight into the current crisis..."

Pushy. Impelled. Yes, that was it.

Rising abruptly – one of the power moves she had learnt in

the training course – and feeling for the baton at the side of hips that Calvin had called *substantial*, Amber when into action, deliberately exaggerating her intonation.

"SIR, like YUH doh UNderSTAND ENG-lish? Yuh CAN-not SEE de ED-di-TOR JUS-so. WE have pro-CEDURES to FOL-low."

She sat down again, keeping eye contact.

"Make an appointment. Come back tomorrow."

Scholar engaged her with a blank stare.

Amber lifted a ledger to seal her point.

"Look. See this book? When yuh get an appointment, upstairs will give the ok to let you in. Now, Mr. Gentleman, leave the building."

"Leave, Miss? Whom am I offending? The matter will be settled with one call to the editor. You could let him know I was a colleague of the late Mr. Sm—"

"SIR!" she spat out the word.

An eruption was brewing; it was time to step up the game. The rule for Taking Control: *Never show your opponent weakness...* but her mind went blank... *never show... weakness...*

She froze. A memory of the last conversation with her father interrupted her flow. He had called out of the blue and she had pretended not to recognize his voice.

"Is me," he said, "Charlo. What happen? Yuh forget your own father? I know time tight with you – but tomorrow I make sixty."

He went silent as though expecting a reaction, but when none came he coughed and went on.

"We could get something to eat. Maybe some Chinese somewhere in town. I know Sando far."

"Tomorrow not good for me. I have to work a double," she lied.

"Ok, no problem. Maybe a nex' time," he replied in a upbeat kind of way.

She had heard the disappointment in his voice, but ended the call with a promise to text if things changed. She should not have been so cold. Maybe he didn't want to be alone. Maybe he wasn't alone. The truth was she didn't want to know.

Scholar had erupted by the time Amber caught herself. He had thrown his arms into the air and with his eyes raised to heaven, he shouted, "You would never allow this atrocity to take place, Smithy. No respect for people. I have an opinion to share! A point of view..."

The man was really mad. What to do? She really did not know.

Cummings and Randolph came from nowhere. In unison they shoved the troublemaker towards the exit.

"Lock the door!" Cummings barked.

The whole place stopped to take in the scene. In a daze, Amber saw the sad pantomime from behind the safety of the building's glass facade. Cummings stood like a wall in front of Scholar who sat with his knees drawn into his chest. He carried on a muted rant, oblivious to the fate of his precious letter, now trampled upon. Then he started to rock, side to side, as if he was in a boat and the sea was rough. Cummings launched into what looked like a serious tongue-lashing. Scholar clasped his ears. As if that wasn't enough, he stretched out like he was on his own bed, kicking his feet, beating his arms and bawling like some bad spirit was riding him.

The commotion went on until Cummings put God out his thoughts and slapped Scholar. Thunder! That was how the sound ricocheted all over Port of Spain. Spectators looked to heaven and then to the question fixed on their neighbours' faces. One or two had the presence of mind to protest. "Security, yuh advantaging de man!" Cummings relented but that slap – those who saw agreed – caused the colossal piece of bad-mind that rooted Scholar to the spot. No matter how they tried, the man could not be moved. Like a complaint that demanded a hearing, he wasn't going anywhere.

Scholar was not a small man. He believed that brainwork required proper nourishment, so he went to great lengths to ensure that he ate well. The country's present wreckage and future possibility were his daily study. Only stamina and belly could open the gate to clear the blockage. So he was one of the regulars at the soup kitchens on both Frederick and Duncan Streets. Sundays were his favourite; he didn't have far to go to find a meal. A set of people was always sharing out food by Tamarind Square, with Columbus keeping watch right next door. Most of the city's street-dwellers gathered there to sprawl off in full view of the *great discoverer*, like some indictment of a history they had not quite escaped – or a present that was in need of a history to blame.

People came from all over the island, meaning well, making sure the poor were not forgotten. They had their reasons: thanks for all sorts of favours – a child passing exams for a *good* school; an operation for cataracts or kidney stones that went well; a court case won over disputed property; a stray-away son or husband who had come back to his senses; a daughter who had finally found a husband; getting the keys to a government house; a job sought and got; escaping somebody's bad prayers; a visa granted to go to the States or Canada.

They brought all kinds of good-good food: macaroni pie, stew chicken, buss-up shot with curry goat, Chinese rice, potato salad, fresh salad and juice too. Everything nicely packaged in tidy boxes, with napkins and forks. Scholar refused nothing, making sure he was well positioned in the line behind every vehicle that stopped and opened up its trunk, even walking with an exaggerated droop of his shoulder to look hungry for the benefit of his benefactors. And he prayed whatever prayers the people wanted him to pray, respectful of whatever God they worshipped. His mottos were simple, not new but true: *One God: Many Paths. Those who give do the work of conscience.*

It was no surprise, then, that the security officers discovered it was a formidable task to get Scholar under control. Realizing that water more than flour, Cummings conceded they needed backup; he called headquarters. One man was available. The curfew had put a strain on personnel. The only option was to lift Scholar bodily into the van. But even with the help of the driver, moving Scholar would still be a problem. There were only three of them. A fourth man was needed, each to take hold of a limb. Someone from the growing crowd would have to do.

That was when Cummings caught sight of Ragga standing tall among the curious spectators, holding a black bottle in his hand. He looked the part.

Ragga was in fact making his way to *The Focus*. Prince's story had to be heard. The paper was sure to be interested, but the big bacchanal in front of the building ended that possibility. He found himself recruited to assist in the operation. At first he didn't want to get involved, but something about the indignity suffered by the man he knew they called Scholar made him change his mind. *The Focus* had closed its doors for the day anyway. The problem of finding a place to store his knapsack was solved when he spotted the lone security officer inside the building, her face pressed to the glass. He gestured to her, pointing to his bag, which he placed by the door.

Amber had not yet recovered her composure. Helping the young man was an opportunity to show a little competence, so she stepped out and tried to pick up the knapsack. She gasped, almost toppled by its weight. Ragga quickly relieved her.

"It good here," he said, placing the bag just inside the door.

Amber nodded her agreement to keep an eye on it, further embarrassed that she could not carry the weight. Three years in the job and until now she'd never really been tested. It had all gone wrong.

"Maybe this work is not for me?"

Without intending, she had spoken her question aloud.

"Could be."

He flashed such an open smile she felt she had made a friend.

With the four men working together, Scholar was hoisted from the pavement, his body spreadeagled and suspended in mid-air like an enormous spider. Moving him to the waiting van was easy enough, but once inside a fresh bout of protests began. Once again flat on his back, he heaved and gasped like a drowning man, straining his neck upwards and filling his mouth over and over again with air until his cheeks looked like they wanted to burst. An unexpected calm fell.

When they thought he had simmered down, Scholar started to blow – HA-AH – AO-HI-AI-HO-AO-EE-AI – HU-OU – until it seemed he had exhausted every vowel and combination he could make, releasing into the air a constellation of sounds, but not a single word. Not words but the pain of their soundings, like a woman in labour pushing out her new born into the waiting world.

The bewildered guards and mesmerised crowd felt a great push forward, through and down, drawn up on the inhale and let down on the exhale. Lungful after lungful of raw unstructured sound, unformed words wanting to be heard.

That was what amazed and frightened them – the realization that they each heard whatever unvoiced need they carried through their days. So when Cummings, as if shaking himself free from some powerful spell, shouted to the driver, "Take him straight St Ann's!" Nobody disagreed. He had brought them much too close to a threatening eye from which they could see themselves. As soon as the driver mashed gas, and the van got on the way, the talk went that a heavy cloud appeared over town, then wind and rain – like when a water bag break. OH!

THE BOY IN THE SUPERMAN T-SHIRT

Runs usually happened once a day, maybe twice, though not always every day, and never at the same time. Chubby liked to mix things up, especially who got picked. If they were lucky, between them Supers and Flash got to run at least twice a week. There were others in the pool, but they did not hang with them. Not all the runners followed the same rules. It was easy enough work – once the runner remained alert – but since the SoE, things had slowed. Too risky.

Toby's job was to bring the word. That meant he chose who got to run. He used to be a runner, but not since the "thing" happened. Ambushed at Chubby's end. Since then he'd stopped hanging with them. Maybe he felt he had gotten a promotion. Maybe he was ashamed. What mattered was that he could not be trusted. He was no longer on their side.

What unnerved the boys was his knack of appearing like a ghost on the Promenade.

"Fellas, special delivery," he said sharply, his changing voice doing an up-and-down dance.

The boys were at one of their usual hangouts, playing go-to-pack in the shade of the trees. They preferred not to stay in the same spot, but that made it difficult for Toby to find them. Moving put the ones they called *sickos* off their trail. Chubby was one. It was a game of chance, but running gave them a shot at handling their own money, and that meant more than just survival.

Their luck was on; Friday was a good day for a run. Sometimes customers gave tips, maybe feeling grateful that they had received their packages. But Toby was in a bad mood. That meant Chubby was edgy.

"'W' today, and doh waste time. No games," he snapped.

Supers and Flash exchanged glances. Supers took his lucky Superman T-shirt from his knapsack and pulled it on. He never ran without it. It was his last remaining item from home, a birthday gift from his mother, but he was never going back. Flash pulled hard on his thumb. They both knew they would have to change their route again, but not today.

They watched Toby hustle across Independence Square and into the KFC outlet at the corner of Broadway. That meant he had enough bills for at least a dinner box. Most times he got the dinner combo. Sometimes they would spy on him through the glass pane of the outlet when they had nothing else to do, because another runner had sealed the job.

Toby's time was running out. The boys knew. Maybe Toby did too. The word on the street was that he had started taking hits. That would have been Chubby's doing. All round, it was bad news – the beginning of the end. Their job was just to run, and they wanted to keep it that way. They had made a pact – to watch each other's backs.

"Who win buying," Flash announced, though the rule had been decided long before.

Supers pointed boastfully at the logo on his Superman jersey. "We done know that is me!"

Flash was eight. It didn't take much for him to get into his role.

"You can't be talking to me," he countered, "Flash could beat anybody, even Bolt!"

He puffed up his chest, and moved about mechanically, like an automated toy.

Flash was really into the game.

"I running Nelson," Supers announced, as they made their way to the starting point at the bottom of Frederick Street.

That meant when they got to Queen Street, Flash would veer left to Edward Street and then north. Supers would swing right to Nelson – exactly eight blocks apart. Both would race to Duke Street. Supers would swing left and Flash turn right onto Duke. They would head towards Frederick again, which was smack in the middle. The finish line was at the corner on each side. The deal was whoever got there first would do the run for Chubby and get paid.

The race was a game of speed they had invented to prepare for Chubby's run. Toby was a constant reminder of that need. The deal was to drop off what was put in the knapsack at the place he named. A twenty was handed over when they returned, together with whatever cold drink and snack they chose from Chubby's well-stacked cooler and cart. It wasn't his operation. He worked for a wholesaler in town – at least that was the word on the ground. He too moved around, changing locations, to which identifying letters had been assigned.

Supers entered the game of getting revved up. He liked his friend to at least enjoy the run. Flash turned his cap backwards and took his mark, eyeing his opponent. He was positioned for take-off, fists closed and arms ready to begin working, but not before taking a last suck of his thumb, a comfort he held onto regardless of how he was teased, and sometimes bullied, if Supers wasn't around. The streets were not easy. Toughness mattered – but speed and smarts – they meant survival.

"On your mark," Flash instructed, "get set," he dipped further into his take-off position, "...GO!"

Flash was off. Supers held back a little, so his pal could get a good lead. He wanted him to have this win. He'd had the last two, so his had been the responsibility to buy the snack-box combo. That meant Flash had gotten the wing, twice in a row, and he was itching to turn the tide.

They operated as a team: one made the delivery, the other played security. They knew that what had happened to Toby could also happen at the delivery end of the run, depending on the customers, especially those "falsey" ones with the heavily tinted high-riders. Sometimes Chubby made deals behind the runners' backs; sometimes, customers plied their own treats in return for favours. The trick was to never enter a vehicle. Drop off and run. They weren't into the extras.

The job of the security was to keep a safe distance and out of sight until the delivery had been made. Flash had watched his back last time. It wasn't foolproof, but it helped them shake the shivers. Things could happen.

Supers had been winning the races because he was trying to keep Flash out of Chubby's way. He had seen the signs – Chubby directing all his conversations to Flash and offering him extra snacks. Supers knew Chubby wasn't interested in him; one day, before a run, he had made that clear.

"So where your little friend today?"

He had refused the bait.

"What happen? Somebody cut out yuh tongue?"

As Supers quickly fitted the knapsack onto his back, he saw Chubby's entire upper body ripple. It was hard to look at his face.

"That going up by Harris," he said drily.

Supers knew he meant the square, the west gate end. He made to shove off.

"Wait, I not done with you. Doh play dotish with me. When I ask you something, answer."

"I ent hear you, Mr. Chubby," Supers replied, but immediately regretted the claim.

"Remember I could cut you fellas off. Things could happen. I know you done spoil from wherever you come from. So be careful. The streets not safe, son."

Supers felt the floor open and he almost wet himself. How could he know?

"Now get the hell out of here," Chubby snapped.

No doubt Chubby had his eyes on Flash, but Supers needed him to win this one.

Flash was fast. So when Supers took Nelson Street he picked up speed. He didn't want Flash to suspect that he had thrown the run by letting him get too much of a lead. But as he crossed George Street, his eye caught sight of someone running, following in his direction. It looked like Toby or maybe Dog. He wasn't sure; he'd only had a glimpse. Why would he be trailing him? He almost broke his stride running into Keeper. He didn't stop. Maybe he was wrong. Maybe his mind was playing tricks on him.

As planned, Flash turned up on his side of Frederick, a few steps ahead of him.

"I tell you, Flash is king. I tell, you!"

He was overjoyed.

"Next time is licks. Jus' watch!" Supers warned, playing the game, but happy to see Flash so elated.

"Today, I buying," he boasted and broke into a run to Chubby's spot.

Supers walked behind, loitering in front of the shops until Flash had strapped on his backpack and headed for Park Street where he swung west. That meant the run was to Victoria Square. Supers took off in the opposite direction, then at Duke ran parallel, expertly dodging pedestrians, knowing well how to outrun his friend. He flew through the southern entrance and found his hiding spot closer to the Park Street side, but with a clear view of the drop-off spot where a white SUV was already parked.

Not long after, Flash appeared. He walked towards the vehicle. The back door on the driver's side opened. The engine was running.

"Don't go in," Supers heard himself saying as he watched, taking comfort in the open door.

No sooner than the backpack had been removed, strong arms gripped him and muzzled him from behind. He was hustled to a waiting car. Chubby had made plans for him. Who else? The rest happened quickly – the brief ride and the smell of new upholstery and something else. He passed out. Afterwards, he lay among whitewashed tombstones afraid to move. The old paralysis had returned. There'd been the scent of the same cologne his mother's new boyfriend wore, the man, much to his mother's chagrin, he refused to call by name. There was only one thing to do. Wait it out.

Back on the Promenade, Supers went to find Flash, but the usual corner seat in the outlet was empty. Had Flash made it back okay? There was one more place to look – their new night hideout in the discarded guard booth at the parking lot. But as he turned around to look, Flash was standing behind him, pulling on his thumb.

"My turn to buy!" he announced triumphantly. "Where you went? I wait for you whole day," he said, sounding hurt.

"Nowhere," Supers answered dejectedly.

"Well I hungry like a horse."

He charged up to the cashier and ordered, "Snack box combo – two."

It began to rain.

STANDING ROOM ONLY

Friday evening. The line held its breath. The Port of Spain Express docked twenty minutes too late for people needing to make the return trip to beat lockdown. Not a soul wanted to be stranded in San Fernando with the clock counting down to nine o'clock, and so far from home. Then the announcement came from somewhere inside the bus, like hijacked hope.

"Standing room only."

Maureen swayed with the sea of bodies crammed four and more abreast in the gap between the boarding gate and the waiting bus, all single-file civility lost in the anxiety to board. Talk travelled down the line that this was the last bus to town. Bodies heaved forward as if by some phantom force. No one relented, enduring the pressure at the jammed entrance, ignoring the drizzle that blew in off the nearby harbour.

"Look where Trini reach," the man ahead of Maureen, grumbled. "Twenty Eleven – SoE democracy is the vote for change? Well, take that. We reach!"

An anonymous steups resounded, its meaning clear – this was not the time or place for politics. One priority existed – to get home. The line had stopped moving. The hopefuls bobbed there, heads up-tilted like people treading water.

Maureen stood on tiptoe, counting the heads in front of her as she gauged her distance from the entrance. She was almost there and could see a man collecting tickets. He had positioned himself at the head of the steps where he leant comfortably against the dashboard so he could both receive tickets and chat with the driver. His shift was over but he had stayed on to play conductor for his replacement, a heavy-set woman who had spiced-up the schoolish blue of her official uniform with an ebony, chin-grazer bob, highlighted in gold, and nail extensions airbrushed in the national colours.

Another surge forward.

"Fadda! Allyuh going to kill meh chile!" a woman in the crowd bellowed and, from somewhere unseen, a child's muffled sobs arose.

The response from the driver-now-conductor was swift. He stopped collecting tickets –an unspoken directive to those hoping to get on board to simmer down. Pushing would not be tolerated. To communicate how much he was in control, and how well he had read the crisis, he turned to chatting up his co-worker. The audible chuckles that passed between them were enough to convince people that compliance was the only chance they had to get on.

After a few more exchanges for the benefit of the chastened line, the woman called out, for all to hear:

"Jus' tear the tickets, man."

Mercifully, he obeyed, resuming his collecting with measured deliberation, melding his twin performances of in-chargeness and lover-boy surrender as the driver looked on. The line was moving again.

Home. With every inch that brought Maureen closer to the door, the ache in her belly grew more insistent. She wanted to get the story, first-hand, about Keeper's arrest. She wanted to hold her children. The whole bacchanal was sure to be on television that night. Twenty-one arrested on Nelson Street, for no other crime than belonging to the place. Maybe there was more in the mortar. Who was to say? She wanted to hear from those who had been there. TV news – that was a different story.

Her mother had already called to tell what she knew.

"Police pile he, Stokey, Tall Man, and some other fellas on a pick-up like they no better than goods. Imagine that! Cart them off to God knows where – maybe the Besson Street station."

Disbelief was ripe in her voice.

"What this country coming to only God could tell. The boys didn't do nothing wrong. And poor Glenroy – his mother tell me that when police reach, he was in his bed in a strong sleep. I can't say if that tru'. Ragga and the others, thank God, they disappear. Only Keeper was there. They put handcuffs on the boy and take him down."

Maureen took it all in, saying little but trying to let her mother know she, too, was carrying the load. She let her talk until her phone ran dead.

For the rest of the day the news throbbed like a wound, but she kept it to herself, cashing the orders of snack and dinner boxes, leg and thigh, breast and wing, extra fries, Coke and Sprite with her usual efficiency, producing the cheery disposition management wanted. *Remember the Colonel's motto: Smile, this is home away from home.* She kept busy, folding napkins and meal boxes for food that she herself refused to eat – too much grease. She didn't change a thing about how she operated, so nobody would have cause to ask her business.

After what seemed an eternity of shuffling towards the door, Maureen stood one person away from the driver-turned-doorkeeper. He took his time receiving and tearing the perforated end of each ticket. Maureen held her composure, her ticket clutched ready for collection. Her turn finally came. He looked directly at her, his grin a deliberate counterpoint to the anxiety on the faces in the line. Without warning, he turned to those already standing in the aisle and boomed, so that Maureen couldn't help but jump, "Everybody step back or this bus not moving!"

The instruction ricocheted up the aisle. "Dress back. Dress back. Allyuh ent hear the man? Make yuhself small."

People obeyed like children, shuffling back, making room

where there was none. Those already seated settled into their good fortune, wavering between amusement and scandal at the chaos they had escaped. A fella, who looked like he ordinarily couldn't mash ants, felt emboldened enough by his luck to chat up Maureen as she squeezed by.

"Ah nice sweets like you shouldn't be standing up in no bus."

Without missing a beat, she fired back, "Well if that is how you really feel, lover, why yuh doh get up and let nice people sit down!"

Sounds of exaggerated surprise rose from the cramped space.

"Wheeeey! Shot call!" someone exclaimed.

"Doh 'fraid to rub it, horse," another joked.

A few fellas nearby burst into raucous laughter. They shielded their eyes and threw themselves back onto each other.

The youth-man withdrew like a moracoy, though he failed to do the heroic thing of giving up his seat. Maureen had already manoeuvred her way further back, not really caring that the bus had acknowledged her victory.

All was forgotten when the word thundered from the front. "Bus full!" The driver-now-conductor exited behind those he had turned back, directing one more muffled intimacy to his replacement, who sucked her teeth affectionately.

The whole bus could hear his banter with those who didn't get on board.

"What allyuh worried about? The government sending another bus." Then for all the bus to hear, his loud "Later" as the automatic door slid shut and airbrakes exhaled.

Passengers allowed themselves to relax, and an easy silence fell, as if everyone wanted to feel in their bodies, without the distraction of talk, that they were really on their way.

Maureen drew her handbag to the front of her body, double-checked to see that it was securely closed, and slipped the strap of her lunch bag over her head – fussing over her possessions in a vain attempt to calm her thoughts: Keeper's new habit of hanging out with Marcus. The man was bad news. There was the extra two thousand Keeper had brought home last month claiming it was his sou-sou hand that had come in. But was that true? In the weeks that followed she had tried to keep silent, not wanting to stir a quarrel when he insisted on paying down on a new living-room set, and started talking about changing that dinosaur of a television not even the labass would want. But saying nothing, she discovered, was the bigger weight. So she let her tongue go.

"I hope yuh not bringing bad money in this house."

"I want better for us, Maureen. That is all I want."

Maureen could not argue with that. They had talked about finding a place of their own.

"I know, Keeper. But we doing okay. One day at a time. I hope yuh not getting in foolishness. Gunman and police doh wait to hear sorry. And, hear me good – I have no argument with the prayers you find solace in. I see what happening. But I know you know that God is no front to hide behind."

The outburst had put a rift between them. Keeper was clearly troubling trouble. They needed to talk. How to handle that?

The bus jolted forward. Maureen grabbed hold of the two adjacent seatbacks to steady herself, only then realizing that she was missing something – her umbrella. A cry escaped.

"Driver, stop the bus!" she shouted and started forcing her way forward. "My umbrella, Drive!"

"Leave the damn thing. People want to go home," someone advised irritably.

But she would not relent, pushing her way through to the front, oblivious to the commotion she was causing.

"Stop the bus!" she pleaded, pointing in distress at the forgotten object, a yellow umbrella against the blue seating in the terminus building.

"Look it on the chair!" she shouted, seeing again Keeper's smile after he had paid the vendor. "That colour is you, girl. Is you," he had said.

"Once *dat* yellow is not a rising sun, I with you," she replied and they had a good laugh at the pun.

"Driver, one minute, please!" she begged.

Maybe some on the bus guessed at her pain, that her distress was much greater than the forgotten umbrella. Something bigger was at stake. Those who understood this took her side, their pleas going ahead of her: "Let the lady get she umbrella. Stop the bus, Drive!"

The demand gathered momentum and advanced like a wave to the front. The driver tipped the brakes, and fixed an inscrutable stare through the passenger mirror at the commotion at the back. The door abruptly jerked open. The smart-mouth youth who had tried to play fresh with Maureen sprang from his seat and pushed his way to the exit.

By the time he got there, the driver-now-conductor was waiting outside the bus with the umbrella extended like an offering. This time, it was the lady-driver who smiled down at him, and crooned, "Later." The youth-man accepted the umbrella and walk backed to Maureen, holding it high like a prize. The whole bus clapped and called him *Hero*. Maureen, a little repentant over how she had embarrassed him, could only say a quiet *thanks.*

When the bus got on its way the second time, the going was smooth and light, with *Hero* smiling broadly in the aisle and Maureen, now sitting in his place, clutching the umbrella to her like it was a love that hadn't been left behind.

MAN DOWN

Marcus draws hard. He closes his eyes... holds... exhales... slowly. Smoke swirls and hangs above him so that the room, with only the light from the television screen, seems a dream he just happens to be awake in... He speaks to the screen as though it is a companion and expects it to answer...

The man is boss. Give him that... Watch movements... Real smart... No chupidy. Bright. Original. Look, how easy that next fool go dead. Technical... Look how he stand up in the open like he asking for lead. Yeah, the brother is ah thinker... Look. He hiding in the mudda-ass trunk... Watch that stylin' from inside the car... Aim and BAM BAM... the stiff eat ground. Cool. Real cool...

The scene changes. He is not interested so he takes a long pull then kills the joint between his thumb and index finger. He pockets the end. In the next scene a boy is doing his homework at a kitchen table. The star saunters in. Words of advice are directed to the boy, his little brother. He announces he is going to work.

Dat is it! ... Check the crib – fresh, chilled.

The frame changes.

Them po-lice so dotish. They cyah catch the man... He too clean... smooth. Now watch how he mash up that hater... feel she hard like gangster. BAM! Double barrel inside the peep-hole… Blow off she face.

He jumps from his seat, grabs his crotch and does his Iwer-style prance and addresses the screen:

Sweet man. Good for she… Shot man! Watch dah nex' one bawling like she man dead. Laaawd!

He sits down again and his cellphone rings to Rihanna singing – Oh Mama, Mama, Mama, I just shot a man down in Central Station… *His index finger stabs at the pause button on the remote. The woman's blown-away face becomes the still that he focuses on while he listens to the caller…*

Yeah, I ready. Jus' make sure your people doh stick. I want my bills like we agree. I know you doh want to see my face.

He slides the cell onto the coffee table. Stares off into nowhere… then abruptly reaches for the remote. The next scene unravels.

This one real sweet. That is how I taking down that next one … digging up in people business. She have belly. I like that. She ent 'fraid nobody…

He pauses, then snaps back as from a far place…

Now watch this… BMX ride then BAM! Classic take-down…

He aims the remote at the screen, presses the stop key and slumps back into the softness of the sofa to stare at the vacant blue as if savouring the nothingness it offers back – or is replaying the last scene in his head. Satisfied by some private triumph, he smiles.

Dread, time to cool down.

He rises and walks over to the window. The drapes are flung open. An expansive view of the Gulf greets him. He considers the scene. The sky threatens rain. He steps backs and takes a shooter's stance, his aim trained on the setting sun.

BAM! And get out, *he says aloud*. I done.

He slowly draws the curtains closed, turns and walks over to the bed where he throws himself down and stretches out. The sheets are smooth, soft, clean... The mattress is king size... air-conditioner is on 20°c... Rihanna starts singing again: Rum bum bum bum, rum bum bum Man Down. *The caller I.D. says Keeper.*

What that yellow sufferer want now? Frig-up the damn run because he want out? It doh wuk so, brother. People expect me to deliver.

He hesitates. Watches the screen until the phone goes silent.

Keeper, my backside. Po-lice feel I born yesterday... Not home! [*He shouts at the screen and laughs at his own joke.*] Maybe the next one is more man. And Keeper, boy, doh put God out yuh thoughts and talk... Is them two girls going down first. But I know yuh know that, brother. I know you know...

He selects a new ring tone.

Sorry, baby-girl, yuh daddy fed-up with that song.

He powers down the phone and lies back again, draws his arms up, holding them vertical for a few seconds... Elbows bent, he locks his fingers behind his head and looks down at the length of his body. Calm envelops him. He sighs and closes his eyes.

He begins to prep himself.

They cyah touch you, Marcus... Them fellas is ah set of mammy-boy cowards. Easy pickings. In and out.

A slow smile grows on his face... and the room fades... Something like frantic clattering pulls him out of sleep – his *phone.*

Yeah. No, I wukking tonight. Busy.

He listens. Silence.

Anyway, lock up tight. Alisha ok? Remember – tomorrow, early, we going by Courts for that set.

Hah-Ayiii...

A frown knits his brow... He draws the phone away from his ear... waits until the laughter fades and says:

Have nothing to say. I tired tell you dat! I fixing my family nice. How I make my money is my business. Who vex lorse!

Laughter from the other end. He muffles the sound in his chest, inhales deeply and looks at the ceiling.

She 'fraid me! My own mudda...

The realisation draws him to sit up. He listens again then abruptly ends the call.

Look, I busy now. Lock up good. I gone...

The bedside clock flips to six. He flings the phone away and wearily draws his palms down his face. His fingers find a spot in the middle of his forehead… He slips to the floor and bows down… Silence… An almost inaudible sound like sobs… Silence… He inhales deeply… rises and moves mechanically towards the dazzling white of the bathroom. He turns on the shower, strips and adjusts the hot and cold taps. Steps in…

Water like warm milk cascades over him. He hangs his head savouring the liquid caress on his shoulders. Pure. Clean. Water.

A REAL CONNECTION

At about the time the storm that washed Port of Spain was in full swing, the Minister of All Things Legal was travelling on the Beetham Highway in the vicinity of Sealots. His driver, Ivan, was going at a speed way above the limit. His boss needed to be at Television House. The entire nation was awaiting his address. He was in danger of running late on account of the unscheduled meeting. A woman had defied the Minister's usually vigilant security detail, claimed to have known him from earlier days when his portfolio was housing, and stopped him in his tracks with a name.

"Sumintra Subir."

The brow crease was instantaneous.

"Sumintra... the one that leave unfinished business," she said, a little louder than necessary. "Remember me now?"

Ivan saw the Minister's lips mime her name and the quick glance at his watch. Impromptu appointments were seldom entertained, and his address to the nation was at eight sharp. Ivan didn't miss the unguarded look of disbelief before he signalled the security officer to relax. The woman followed the Minister into the building with an uplifted head, her gait almost triumphant.

"Trouble," Ivan thought.

The encounter had surprised him. He was left holding the opened door of the Prado in anticipation of the Minister's departure. Miss Subir had come prepared to wait for him. She held an umbrella and a folding chair. His presence at the San Fernando office that day had been highly publicized. There were emergencies at hand that needed his attention. The people needed reassuring that he was on the job.

After the better part of an hour, the Minister emerged from the building. Ivan could see he was more than a little ruffled from the way he flung himself into the vehicle. He furtively considered his passenger's irate and sulky face.

"Drive," the Minister snapped.

"Cocoa in the sun," Ivan murmured and put the SUV into gear.

Now, he had to drive above his usual speed to get to the studio on time. He didn't want to disappoint. But as they neared the city – more rain, wind and lightning. Traffic was sure to be backed up on Wrightson Road, so he decided to take the turn-off at the Sealots lighthouse onto Broadway. His plan was to swing up Richmond to the Savannah and onto Marli by the Embassy. Television House was at the western end. Easy.

He was lucky to get the green light at the lighthouse exit. The vehicle was in a full left swing onto South Quay from the old railway station and he was half-listening to the Minister rehearse his speech. Later, he would remember being more than a little baffled that the ace in the address was the *serious matter* of a breach of national security perpetrated by some delinquent teenager on the world-wide-web. Criminal elements clearly needed to be weeded out from all quarters.

That was when the trouble began. Ivan's vision was obstructed by a piece of cardboard that alighted on the windscreen. In the heavy downpour it stuck there, causing him to brake suddenly and spin out of control. The Prado did a complete 360 or two, then veered east towards the traffic lights at the pedestrian crossing. It swung around again, righted itself and came to an abrupt halt facing west.

"What the hell!"

"Sorry, Boss," Ivan offered quickly.

No response came from the back.

The rearview mirror told him why. The Minister was bent over collecting the scattered pages of his speech. He had seen nothing of the piece of cardboard or the angry pedestrians pointing accusing fingers at the Prado.

To launch into excuses was not a good idea – Ivan knew the man – but he had something else on his mind. He had definitely seen something – a name boldly written, but with the self-consciousness of a child: Ignatius Rakesh Ramlochan, B.A. M.A. of the People's Parliament.

The initials I.R.R. were written in the one thing he possessed from the man he had been told was his father: a copy of *The Tale of Two Cities.* He kept the book among his personal belongings – though he'd never managed to read it through to the end. Nothing about the story had captured him as much as the opening lines, words that had stuck in his mind, almost like a mantra, that now came back to him:

> It was the best of times, it was the worst of times, it was the age of wisdom, it was the age of foolishness, it was the epoch of belief, it was the epoch of incredulity, it was the season of Light, it was the season of Darkness, it was the spring of hope, it was the winter of despair, we had everything before us, we had nothing before us, we were all going direct to Heaven, we were all going direct the other way...

The Minister surfaced, papers in his hand.

"Boy, you trying to kill me or what!"

Just then a gust whisked away the bit of trash as quickly as it had been delivered.

The Minister cleared his throat. "I hope you're not drinking on the job, Ivan?"

The question was tempered with the right degree of concern so as not to come across as blatantly accusing.

"Not me, boss."

Uncertain as to whether his reply would seem too absolute to be true, he added, "Well weekend... maybe one or two beers. That is all."

The eye contact he was allowed told him that being shaken up so close to his appearance on national television was not at all appreciated.

"My job not easy, son – holding the scales of justice in balance, especially when the country is in crisis. From six in morning, even before the nation's rubbish is collected, I am at the people's service. You understand what I'm saying, boy?"

The Minister leaned back into the comfort of new leather. Ivan knew better than to suggest that his boss was wrong. It kept things pleasant. He concentrated on his driving, only to be startled by what sounded like an explosion. The Minister had slammed his briefcase shut. Ivan's hand accidentally hit the horn.

"You better not be drinking on the job. I will fire yuh ass! Too much bad rumour spreading about what should not be happening inside government vehicles. I won't be implicated!"

"Sorry Boss. I swear. I doh drink at all."

No response but the agitated shuffle of papers.

Cautiously, he set the vehicle in motion, but the response of the SUV's powerful engine to the pressure he applied to the accelerator only fuelled his resentment. He had betrayed himself. That was a fact. He began targeting every pothole. Each strike compensated for the small truth he had failed to defend: his vision had been impaired.

To no avail. The Minister was much too preoccupied with his speech to be bothered. Defeated again, Ivan switched to an exercise in the avoidance of every cavity and bump in the road, going at a snail's pace, until it occurred to him that he was searching for the apology he needed to offer himself for allowing the Minister to rob him of his truth. It had happened again. What he did in his free time was his own business. He wasn't a child. The problem was his. He readjusted his driving.

There was one thing about his boss that Ivan respected – though not enough to really admire him. He was supportive of anyone committed to making a fresh start, "pulling themselves up by the boot straps." Weakness produced no rewards. Life only gave what a person was willing to fight for. The idea was as discomforting as it was attractive. Not that he believed living should be an easy street, but the Minister had a different notion about what was permitted in the fight. He had worked with him long enough to know that much. Nothing stopped *him* getting what he wanted. The sisters at the orphanage had given Ivan a different perspective.

Life wasn't some enemy to be conquered. You had to allow it to lift you up – like a father carries his child on his shoulders, so the whole view ahead, with all its possibilities, was visible, reachable simply because it was there. You didn't have to bulldoze a place or walk over people to get it. Maybe everyone needed some kind of uplift. That was the nuns' view – the ones that shone. Deep down, they knew who they were and believed a greater source lifted them up. There was no need to grasp like a greedy child or, for that matter, to live like an orphan. But was that enough? Fight. He felt had to fight *his* fight.

"That is it, man! That is it!" he exclaimed.

A light had been switched on.

"You said something? We almost there?" the Minister asked distractedly.

"We on Marli now," Ivan answered, but his mind was elsewhere – on the name he had seen on the renegade cardboard – Ignatius Rakesh Ramlochan – the name of his father, the man who had too much brains for his head...

"Book-learning never hurt nobody, but Iggy had ideas people were not ready for. He believe that his business was to fight for every Tom, Dick and Harry."

That was always how she began her story, the one aunt on his father's side who paid him a yearly visit at Christmas, coming all the way to the orphanage in Belmont with her gift of a grey blanket and a red apple. She sat, self-consciously upright on the wooden bench in the visitors' room, looking like she was ready to leave as soon as she had arrived. Ivan listened to her with his eyes cast down on his rubber slippers. As uncomfortable as they were, her visits were the only chance to piece together the puzzle of who he was and the people he had come from.

"Your mother, she wasn't from here – small island, yuh understand? She wasn't even from our side."

She repeated these lines like a personal disappointment every time.

That was all she ever said of his mother, that she was an outsider in ways he could not comprehend. She had died in childbirth, and later they had to take him from the father he could barely remember because he had become a St Ann's regular. No one in the family had come forward to claim him. He wasn't their business.

As he grew older, the puzzle got even more disconcerting. If his mother wasn't from his father's side or from his place, then to what side did she belong, and where did that leave him? The only solution he could come up with was that he was the island where he was born – Trini, that was his only side and his place.

"The problem with Iggy was that he didn't know where to draw the line. Shouting *Power* in the people streets. And look where all that marching get him. Yuh understand me, boy?"

The last time she visited, it was mango season. She was going away and had come with a gift, the book that was his only inheritance – that and the bits of conversation he remembered. Most of it had gone over his head.

Nothing of those stories Ivan could prove or disprove. All he had was an uncanny sense that this stranger was trying to connect with him – after all these years. So he did the oddest thing. Once the Minister of All Things Legal had alighted from the vehicle at the television station, Ivan parked the Prado and gave the keys to the security at the booth with some bogus excuse. The Minister could find his own way home.

THE ACCIDENT

Amber switched between channels hoping to catch a report of the accident at South Quay that evening. She had gotten home too late to catch *Crime Time*. Mr. Lane was sure to have carried a version. Only NTT had a short clip, but the writer didn't get the story quite right. Somebody, an anonymous eyewitness, had captured the event on a cellphone camera and sent it in at the last minute. The station deemed the incident a suitable preface to the highly anticipated eight o'clock address from the Minister of All Things Legal. She soon saw why. There was a connection, another chapter in the general bacchanal of the place. The station, at least, wanted to make that point.

Even so, the coverage of the Prado incident was obviously a rushed production. It showed the woman – who the nation came to know as Beatrice Monsegue of Belmont, a regular participant in the protests staged outside the parliament building – belly down on the pedestrian crossing at the South Quay and Broadway intersection. Spliced-in rather comically in the distant background was an SUV dangerously tilted to one side, too far away for the plates to be deciphered. What seemed to be the news was that the woman was purportedly a distant relative of a financial magnate embroiled in a legal battle with a whole set of policyholders who wanted his head.

It troubled Amber that the woman's spurious family ties – even if correct – took precedence over the role of the Prado in the incident. She had witnessed the entire thing. There must be something behind the clever relegation of the vehicle to the edge of the frame, but she had no evidence. Maybe that was the point. Presented to the public in this way, the woman's fate seemed like some crude brand of justice – the only one that would ever be exercised against the wrongdoings perpetrated by the maverick relative who had managed to locate himself beyond the law. Protests, audits and inquiries had failed to pin responsibility for the embezzlement of people's money on anyone. The whole global economy was in a mess. Investments were risky. Let taxpayers' money bail out the company. There had to be a name for that – no matter what government handled the bail-out.

Amber wondered, too, about the Scholar fiasco at *The Focus.* Had she handled it differently, his eruption might have been avoided. But that was water under the bridge. Nothing of that incident had made the spotlight. Madman dramas were perhaps too common in Port of Spain to be considered prime news. Probably the media had its own way of avoiding national scrutiny... or getting on the wrong side of the powers that be. Things were that bad in the place. Mr. Lane's show would have helped fill a gap – even as entertainment. Calvin's anthem rang in her head as she curled up on the couch waiting for the Minister to appear on the screen.

"Facts, girl. That is the only thing between us and fiction. Other than that, all we doing is acting. Just like Valentino sing, we on a stage. Give me a fact. That is when I know what I'm dealing with."

It suddenly occurred to her that she and Calvin were stuck. He could offer her nothing concrete. That was the understanding he wanted her to accept. Six months along and it was already clear. They weren't going anywhere, and maybe that was what he had been trying to say all along under all the head games he played, and she foolishly enabled.

"But not every thing we could weigh and measure. Who is the keeper of your facts, Calvin?"

"So what yuh really saying? A person can't get a simple truth out there? Two plus two. There is a solution to that, you know. People complicating simple things for no reason other than they prefer the benefits of the lie."

"Sums and people can't compare, Calvin. You well know that. People living inside two maybe three stories. So life stop. That don't make it right. If you ask me, you 'fraid to admit that because you too tied up for your own good."

"'Fraid... ? That mess out there has nothing to do with me, Amber. I just doing my job."

"Who say I talking about what going on out there? Everybody 'fraid something, Calvin. That is all I mean."

Amber didn't push him further. Who was she to demand better from him? They both shared in the wrong that needed to be put right again.

She turned her thoughts to the South Quay story. The glaring omission bothered her. She had seen the whole thing from under the eaves of *The Jewellery King,* where she'd been waiting for the traffic lights to change. Her mind was full. At the very moment the Prado lost control, she was wondering where Calvin was; regretting she had not returned her father's call and agreed to meet him for lunch; and feeling more than a little embarrassed at how she had handled the madman affair. It would not look good on her record, and Cummings would not spare her.

"This job is not for weaklings and cowards," he'd smirked.

Amber hadn't answered, though weak was not a self-description she harboured. She had dug her way out of the mourning house her mother had presided over, nursing her loss of Charlo with a violent victimhood that made her lash out at the world, slapping it in the face every day. And there was Marcus and his colossal anger that nobody could account for, his moving through the place like he had a score, older than history, to settle.

Survival she knew about, but she wasn't the coward Cummings suggested. Years of negotiating her way through the shards of her mother's wounded pride and the black hole that was swallowing her brother had toughened her spirit. But the man, Scholar, had unnerved her, his unbridled shouting, spit flying from his mouth and clinging to his beard. He was force and vulnerability, clarity and confusion, beauty and horror, all at once. She could not find a path through that collapse of borders.

No. Her day hadn't ended well, and on top of the incident with Scholar, Gooding had failed to turn up for his shift. That gave Cummings another chance to play hero and put her down. With her more than questionable performance, and with the whole country in lockdown, he had no choice but to take up the slack.

"Sweetheart, you not up to do a double today," he had said, his voice oiled with condescension. He stepped back to study her face. "Go home."

The decision struck her like a thunderbolt, but she managed not to let on. She had failed to act. Cummings would make her pay for it. He was sure to recommend a transfer, if not more.

"Not good," she repeated to herself. "Not good."

Her arrival at South Quay had coincided with the exit of the passengers from the San Fernando Express. The bus had docked in its usual spot in front of the old railway station. Rain fell like peas so the drains were full and the streets would soon be an impassable sea. While many people huddled in dismay under any available eave, others, ignoring the traffic lights, attempted daring athletic leaps across the street to the terminus.

It was not clear to Amber whether Beatrice Monsegue had been on the bus. When she emerged from behind the parked vehicle, she trailed a woman with an upheld yellow umbrella. They moved with the stream of people heading for the nearby pedestrian crossing. This was exactly when the ministerial vehicle – she definitely saw the plates – swung onto South Quay at a speed too fast for taking corners, particularly in bad weather.

Beatrice followed behind the pedestrians as they negotiated their way through the rising water. A moment's hesitation would risk being stranded at the Priority. They had come much too far to be further detained. Thank goodness the woman was agile. Catching sight of the runaway Prado that was heading her way, she bravely threw herself forward just in time to avoid being run over as the vehicle spun into its second or third rotation. The dash sent her flying across the wet asphalt, causing a collision with the woman ahead of her who started forward. Although she managed to keep her balance, she lost her hold of the umbrella. It caught the wind and swirled up like an ecstatic butterfly to join the dance of what looked like a piece of windswept cardboard.

Many of the onlookers were so taken by the spectacle that Beatrice was momentarily forgotten; those that remained attentive to her plight held their breaths as the parcel she carried broke free of her grip and joined the rushing of water in the swollen drain. In what seemed like a split second, Beatrice was on her feet, oblivious to her bruised elbows and knees. A cry of distress that seemed oceans' deep rang out.

"O Lord, Ganga! The fish – it gone!"

Amber was among those who had rushed to help the woman; she recognised her as one of the nation's lone-wolf activists. The owner of the umbrella, with tears welled-up in her eyes, started to push back the crowd shouting, "Give the lady air!"

In the ramble that came from the distraught woman, Amber gathered that it was not the fall, but the lost parcel of fish that was the cause of her inconsolable grief. Deaf to the words of consolation about her broken tooth, a sign people agreed was not at all good, and ignoring the queries about calling an ambulance, Beatrice arranged her soaked clothes and limped away, mumbling something about, "Poor Ganga."

Amber could not confirm it. She was busy helping to steady Beatrice on her feet, but someone claimed to have seen the fish gleefully beat its tail as soon as it hit the water that gushed towards the Gulf.

LADY, YOU OKAY?

Even from across the street, Maureen could see that the woman standing, soaked to the bone, at the corner of Henry and Independence Square was in trouble. Amidst the press of bodies, she looked wildly about her as if uncertain of what to do or where to go. No one paid her any attention. Nothing was more important than finding a transport that would get them out of the rain and on their way to wherever was home.

Home too was on Maureen's mind. She was tempted to hurry on, but the woman's obvious anguish brought back her own moment of panic at the pedestrian crossing at Broadway when her beloved umbrella escaped her hold and went spiralling up and away in the wind. Her thoughts shifted again to Keeper. Whatever his story, they would tackle the arrest together. She hoped he felt the same – that they could work things out. She wasn't going anywhere.

"We good together, Keeper," she had said.

The morning had still been new. They lay listening to each other's breathing. She could sense his wanting to say something, but instead he reached for her and she let him draw her close, their foreheads touching ever so slightly in the half-light. Her gratitude registered as a soft glow in her belly, like someone had turned on a light in there. She knew he was offering an apology and kissed his lips in acceptance. Nothing said. No need for words. He slipped out of bed to begin his routine of preparing the girls' clothes and lunch kits. It was a duty he had made his own, so she could get a few more minutes' rest before getting ready to catch the bus to

San Fernando. It was going to be a long day. She had signed up for a double. One of the evening shift cashiers had called in sick.

"That nonsense have to stop, Maureen," Keeper complained.

She hadn't replied immediately, sensing that he was more upset about her questions about the extra money he had brought home. His sou-sou-hand story didn't fly. After her initial outburst, she had allowed things to simmer down. For days they circled the truth she had spoken.

"We have to talk, Keeper. You know that?"

He had looked away with something like sadness on his face and stormed out without saying where he was going.

"Yes, we really have to talk, Mr. Keeper," Maureen repeated as she approached the stranger at the corner.

Something was definitely wrong.

"Lady, you okay?"

Maureen could see that she was not in her element. She was clearly accustomed to dressing and looking fancy, but under the shadow of the eve at Church's Chicken, her floral patterned cotton dress looked like a piece of soggy drapery. Hair fell like a frizzled veil over her face, and behind that tattered screen, her eyes were blotched by mascara. The thought crossed her mind, with some amusement, that the government had missed the boat. The SoE should have been declared for Trini women in distress.

"You need help?" she pressed, realizing that her first question had not registered.

"I need to go," the woman pleaded through gritted teeth.

That explained the discomfort etched on her face. There was no masking the urgency.

"I can't hold it any more."

"What, yuh have to pee?"

Her quick head-shake and glance at her feet said everything.

"Oh-ho!" Maureen intoned.

There was something vaguely familiar about the woman,

but in the turmoil of her emergency, Maureen made no effort to pursue the fleeting connection. The situation was grave. She took charge. Everywhere was closed – even the priests' place across from the Cathedral. Moreover, the water was almost knee high on that side of the Promenade. She had managed to cross at the Cipriani Roundabout, but not without having to wade through the water in full view of her ever-smiling, white-bearded boss, the Colonel.

"I living up Nelson," she said, having concluded that there were no other options. "You could go there, if you want. Is up to you."

The lady seemed both surprised and terrified at the offer. She threw her eyes in the direction of Nelson Street.

"Not far – just over there," Maureen offered, looking directly at the woman, in the hope that she would see her own urgency to get home.

The woman groaned and doubled over.

"I can't wait. I really have to go."

On the insistency of that need, Maureen held the lady by the elbow and hustled her along the pavement, past the Cathedral and across to Tamarind Square. It was understandably deserted. The usual residents had been forced to seek shelter from the rain and the approaching curfew. Maureen guided her to the most sheltered area of the grounds.

"You mean here?

The woman looked about her nervously. Nearby, Columbus loomed serene and washed under the heavy sky. The statue and the entire grounds had benefited from a recent improvement project. The Spanish royal family was due for a visit. The government wanted the place to look *world class*. So Columbus, too, deserved a touch-up. Perhaps the message that gesture hoped to convey was that the nation had long surpassed his part in its beginnings. There were no longer any hard feelings on that score. The republic was charting its own course. True.

The woman nervously assessed the area. What else to do?

"You mean in the grass?"

Maureen knew better than to enter into a useless debate. The gripe would soon answer, but the woman had a point. A quick scan of the area revealed a discarded plastic bag caught in the new sweet-lime hedge.

"Here. Look, I have plenty napkins."

She hastily extracted from her bag a take-home supply branded with the Colonel's face.

"Go ahead, I standing watch," she encouraged.

The lady looked disbelieving.

"Go on. No shame in that. Is an emergency."

That last offering did the trick.

Maureen turned her back and did exactly what she promised – stood guard while the woman emptied herself, finding almost instant relief from the mysterious gripe that had taken hold of her in the middle of town.

The last time she had done anything like that was behind some cars one Panorama Sunday – a long time ago. She had gone on her first real date with Vincent to listen to the steelbands practice their tunes on the barber-green. He worked in the copy department of the small insurance firm she had landed a job with after the ordeal of sixth form was over. He was a self-reliant, even-tempered sort who preferred to do rather than talk; the star striker on the *Motor Guard* team, whose self-effacing manner was quite possibly the source of his ability to electrify the football field with his dazzling plays. He was a new man and maybe that was why they called him Prince.

The "date", which later became a joke between them, was her initiative. He was shredding documents in the copy room when the invitation surfaced.

"So I hear you going away," he had said.

"Yes. This August."

"Where?"

"London. A Bachelor's in Education."

They both spoke in staccatos.

"Real good. Good. I leaving just now, too. Starting my own business."

"Oh yes!" she said. "What's that?"

Her enthusiasm must have encouraged him.

"Small construction and transport. Tiling, cupboards – that is my thing. All now I doing it on the side, but I want to break out in full."

A long pause followed. He didn't seem to know how to go forward, so she decided to break the ice.

"You like pan?" she asked.

"Yeah. You?"

"Want to meet up by the savannah, Saturday?"

They agreed. She would meet him at the top of Cipriani Boulevard. It was a short walk from Rogers Street.

She had told Great Aunt Eleanor that she was going on an office lime. They were fairly regular – after-work get-togethers to eat Chinese or see a movie, and beach or river trips on public holidays. She had felt it necessary to lie. Something in her aunt's manner – never blatant, only escaping her in unguarded moments – revealed an unspoken adherence to a social divide. Instinctively, she knew that someone like Prince would cross that invisible line.

It must have been the beer. In the middle of Renegade's run, she found that she wanted to go, but the lines to the bathrooms were long. She couldn't hold, so Prince stood guard after quelling her reluctance.

"Girl," he laughed, "relax! This savannah won't tell a soul. And to besides, this is Carnival. Free yuhself."

When he walked her home, climbing the short flight of steps a little reluctantly, his hands thrust deep into his pockets, Aunt was sitting in the wooden rocker. Massive breadfruit ferns that hung along the length of the veranda thickened the shadow in which she sat. Mavis almost jumped. Prince sensed her surprise and tried to lighten things.

"Pleasant good night, Mother. Vincent is the name."

She didn't acknowledge his greeting, but as the gate clicked shut, announcing his departure, she said, "Get rid of him," and retreated into the gloom of the house, leaving the front door ever so slightly ajar.

Her aunt was the "good-good lady" the priest always took time to say a few extra words to after the service. The good-good lady who had stepped in when her mother's *mistake* turned out bad in the gloomy front room of that very house, where the same bleached picture of the Sacred Heart hung over the front door. Her mother had not lasted three weeks after the delivery; there'd been complications. The whole story was a mystery. All she knew was that something had reared its head the night she came up the steps with Prince and forever changed the way she saw her aunt.

Now, after all those years, she was doing her business again in public.

"Not to worry. It could happen to anybody," Maureen repeated.

Embarrassment clouded the lady's face.

"How far is home? Yuh want to come by me?"

The lady hesitated.

"Nothing to 'fraid. You could call your people from there. Everything going to work out."

Just when she figured that the crisis was over, without warning, like a banshee with a death to grieve, the lady burst out in a wail, sobbing uncontrollably in the darkness of the park.

"Oh Lord, lady, it have nothing to cry so for. Come by me and bathe and eat something. After, we will figure out how to get you home."

They crossed to the northern side of the street in silence, walking slowly, arms hooked, both locked in their own thoughts. Maureen still couldn't place the lady, but foremost in her mind was the need to hear about everything that had happened to Keeper from her mother. She wanted to draw her babies close.

Before they turned to take Nelson, she stopped.

"By the way, I don't even know your name. Mine is Maureen."

"Mavis," the lady replied.

Then she knew.

A MAXI NAMED REDEMPTION

Nothing was clear to Ivan except that the storm had invited a connection. His first instinct was to make his way back to the scene of the skid. He had to begin somewhere.

On Tragarete Road, a mini van, heading east, with the word REDEMPTION written across the upper portion of its windscreen pulled up beside him before he even had the chance to flag it down.

"Town, soldier?"

The driver stretched all the way across the passenger side to roll down the window. A black duffle bag occupied the jump seat.

Ivan could hear the wipers working back and forth, like a metronome. Marley's *One Love* played through the speakers.

"I going Port of Spain," the driver announced, as though feeling it necessary to clarify his destination.

The vehicle wasn't licensed for hire, but Ivan seized the chance to get out of the dark and rain. After a bit of a tug, the door to the passengers' compartment ground painfully open. The cabin was empty. That made him comfortable. He needed to unwind. His decision to abandon the Minister had not yet sunk in. What now?

"Terence is the name," the driver offered good-naturedly as he fiddled with the fingertip lever and pumped the clutch in an effort to get the vehicle into gear.

"Police troubling people for no reason in town. They say bandit riding solo to slip by the law. These days the way easier with company, if yuh know what I mean."

So Terence wasn't just doing him a favour. The van smelt

of bodies that were no longer there. He surmised that the man's PH stint was over.

"Jus' come from Carenage. Everywhere is water. That is rain, eh?"

He glanced over his shoulder.

Ivan offered a nod and rubbed his palms together.

"Yeah, plenty rain," Terence repeated, this time trying to connect with Ivan through the rearview mirror.

"Fuh sure," Ivan quickly returned, and concentrated on peering through the window he had slid open for air. Being looked at indirectly wasn't at all comfortable.

Traffic flowed easily towards the city until they got to Lapeyrouse cemetery where cars crawled towards the Dundonald and Richmond Streets junction. Marley sang on as Terence negotiated the pile-up at the intersection. *Won't you help me sing... All I ever had...* He sang along, obviously energized by the challenge presented by the web of vehicles caught in the middle of the intersection between traffic signals.

Terence was riveted to his private battle with the steering and gears. Drivers blew their horns in exasperation as he took advantage of every opportunity to advance. Their protests only fuelled his efforts.

"Allyuh feel I buy my license," he announced to no one in particular as he came to an abrupt stop, leaving only enough space from the vehicle in front of him for the breeze to pass.

He gave a triumphant glance back at his passenger. Ivan avoided the connection he sought, choosing to offer his thoughts on Terence's driving through his rhythmic nods to Marley's *Who the cap fit...* Let the silence do the talking. It was a skill he had developed from driving the Minister.

"Jah! Is not yesterday I start to drive!" Terence exclaimed.

They were now in the line of traffic heading down Richmond. Without missing a beat, he asked his passenger, "Yuh does watch *Crime Time*?"

Ivan shook his head. His irregular work hours seldom permitted the luxury of watching television on evenings.

"I doh miss it. The man doh make joke with facts."

The mini television that had somehow been mounted onto the dashboard drew Ivan's notice. He was certain the set-up was not legal and wondered if the man was always charged with so such nervous energy.

"Check it out," Terence encouraged, glancing intermittently at the screen while he followed the flow of traffic to Independence Square. He was proud of the contraption, though the picture wasn't as good as the sound that fed through the boom boxes at the back of the van.

"High powered," he boasted and adjusted the antenna. "A pardner install the whole thing. Ragga – he could hook up any kinda system. And he charge decent."

On the screen, the host, Timothy Lane, flamboyant in a floral printed shirt, tangerine trousers and white-framed spectacles, talked and moved about the set like a runaway train. He was in the middle of preparing his audience for a clip he felt would prove to be a comment – by nature itself – on the state of the nation. His topic was, of course, the freak storm.

"That man is something else," Terence exclaimed approvingly.

Mr. Lane had developed, in a very short time, quite a reputation. He had succeeded in marketing himself to viewers as a fearless, straight-talking investigative journalist and television host, committed to shedding light on corruption in any quarter. His self-proclaimed mission was to seek justice for the voiceless and disadvantaged. His audience looked to him not so much for the uncensored, unadulterated facts he claimed to deliver; they craved more the deliciously addictive entertainment that came with the pretence that such a thing was actually possible.

That was his attraction. For the privilege of feeling that they were privy to those elusive facts, audiences were willing to be hoodwinked by his fictions. A fair trade. A fella even sang a calypso praising the work he was doing – and won King. Lane himself was satisfied with the arrangement. He had a role to play.

So when the freak storm hit the island that day, he decided it would provide good footage to weave into a storyline unearthed by one of his undercover investigators in Port of Spain. The talk on the Promenade was that a madman had called down the storm to protest his unjustified rough handling by the security guards employed at *The Focus*. Losing no time, Lane had rushed with his crew to the Lady Young Lookout, intending, for dramatic effect, to open his coverage of the incident with an elevated view of the rain-washed city in the background. He got much more than he had bargained for.

In the thick of a report, staged to capture him cloaked in a Mackintosh at the mercy of the strong winds and torrential showers – an idea borrowed from CNN reporters – the piece of cardboard that had blinded Ivan at the South Quay intersection hovered in the background for a few seconds. The writing was in a hand large enough for viewers to catch the punch line before the wind swept it away again. In case the message was missed, Mr. Lane froze the frame and read it: *People, Use Your Brains: Time for Change.* The initials I.R.R. were at the end.

Ivan couldn't believe his eyes. He bolted forward.

"Drive, turn up the volume."

"No problem. See what I tell yuh. The man doh make joke. Straight up."

But the clip was over and Mr. Lane was saying, "Ladies and gentlemen, you know me. I give you the facts as I get them… and the gentleman who wrote this message is a citizen. People know him from Woodford Square as a peaceful fella – an ideas man. And he was unjustly treated, according to reliable eyewitnesses, only because he had a message to give…"

Without warning the screen went dead.

"What happen? Jus-so!" Ivan protested.

"Like something blow," Terence said, clearly puzzled.

After a few attempts at switching the set on and off, checking the antenna and tapping the frame, he gave up and went back to Marley … *Who the cap fit, let them wear it…* Once again relaxed in his seat and using the duffle bag as an armrest, he declared, "Marley is forever, man!"

They had swung onto Independence Square. Ivan's thoughts were in overdrive. He had gotten what he needed. Like a miracle, life had opened another door.

"Put me down here, brother!"

The request surprised Terence.

"Yuh sure? I reaching as far as Broadway and up Duncan."

"Yeh, I good here. Thanks brother. Thanks!"

"No scene."

The van moved off leaving a cloud of diesel exhaust behind.

Woodford Square. That was Ivan's first clue. Abercromby Street would get him there.

A LITTLE RUNAWAY

Mavis was convinced that once she had spoken her name, Maureen quickened her steps towards home. Her little runaway that morning had turned into quite a muddle. She anticipated another storm at home when she returned, but apart from the episode in the square, she had no real regrets about the day. Something was happening. She couldn't say what, only that as the Prado moved off that morning, the feeling came: it was time for a change.

The Minister wanted fish for dinner – her excuse for an exit.

"Soon be back," she had called to Claudia on her way out.

"Okay, watch the road, M'am."

After what seemed a timed break, she added, "And don't forget the phone, M'am."

It was enough to let her know that Claudia anticipated a late return. She had been with them for years, since Randal and Brenda were in diapers. She could read the signs. It was going to be one of those all-day errands that featured the forgotten cellphone, the alibi that prevented her from checking in to explain her delay. At the automatic gate, Fred nodded in his pleasant way and checked his watch. Round-the-clock security – her husband had insisted on it. Claudia, she suspected, fed Fred generously on more than the daily meals she prepared – it was the little extra cost of hired help. She returned the smile.

"*...run away!*" That was her song as she drove towards the city in the easier flow of mid-morning traffic. It was a keepsake from her first years of work, before London when her life really changed. She kept it as a marker for that time.

"*Girl, run away! Cat does run away...*" So Prince had teased her, after the veranda incident, with one of the season's favourites. She could still see him dancing on the spot, the fluid side-to-side motion of his body marking time as he addressed the lyrics to her. They had never spoken directly about her great aunt; Francine's calypso was a way of clearing the air. So every time he brought up the proposal of a lime without the office as a cover, he would chime, "*...Cat does run away. Dog does run away...*"

It took her weeks to respond to his challenge, but when she finally did, those words became their private joke for how they ended up at Maracas Bay and Granville, and one Saturday, at Store Bay when she had called home with the lie that the group had missed the boat back. There was also the day they skipped work so she could play general go-getter while he finished tiling his mother's living room for her birthday. At the end, when they sat on the little veranda, dusty and sweaty, but happy to share the view of the Gulf it offered, they simultaneously cried out, "Run away" when his mother served them each a bowl of thick beef-bone soup.

That morning *Runs Man* had given her a clear sign. As Port of Spain came into view, she could hear the Minister's voice interrogating and lecturing Claudia if he happened to call home while she was still out.

"Gone where? I tired talk. This place not safe – read the news! Like she forget what work I in!"

Her imagined defence spilled out in the empty car: "Nonsense! A prisoner in my own country? That is where we reach? And what is your response – more security?"

"That is your problem, Mavis – always living in a dream. Criminals roaming this land. Self-protect, self-protect... when on earth will you understand!"

The city beyond Charlotte Street was a stranger to her –

somewhere you drove through on the way to somewhere else. Even in her youth, it marked her furthest trek east of Frederick Street. She had never bothered to test the warnings about the dangers *behind there*, but would often dreevay through the city after the convent let them out, soaking in the life, before Rogers Street and its own schedule of evening rosary, dinner, homework and sleep.

So as the two-storey apartment buildings on Nelson Street came into view, Mavis felt a surge of discomfort. Night was not really the time to make their acquaintance. She followed closely Maureen's brisk pace, listening to her mantra, "Lordie-Lord, what trouble..." surface from another place of anxiety as she hustled along the deserted street. Mavis heard in it an echo of her own alarm that her harmless escape had taken an unusual twist, had chosen to go its own way.

That morning, she had felt that luck was on her side in finding a spot at the NIPDEC car park. Her plan was to make her day a long, leisurely walk from the bottom of Frederick Street up to the savannah and back. She had not done that in years. It ought to have been a straightforward mission, but given the SoE and the public resentment it had stirred, perhaps not without risk. She was careful not to reveal her position at home, but she felt the pushback was not unwarranted. Democracy, thankfully, was still at work. That signal, coming from the guts of the people, drove her desire to feel again the pulse of the streets. A life was there, a real belonging she had begun to touch in the years she had spent at *Motor Guard*. Since then she had been set apart for too long.

The city, for a Friday, lacked its usual buzz. The emergency had obviously kept people away. She took her time, flowing into shops and arcades and checking out the showcases. At about noon she wandered into Woodford Square where she lingered, out of curiosity, to catch the speech of a man dressed in a mismatched suit and generously cheered on as "Scholar" by his handful of enthusiastic supporters. His topic was of course the curfew. By two o'clock, after a few more diversions and rest-stops, she was crossing over to Memorial Park with the sandwich she had purchased on a whim at the *Living Faith* cafeteria.

Where the park opened out like a gateway onto the savannah, she found a bench facing west, and sat in the ample shade of a broad flamboyant, not thinking, just people-watching as she bit into her sandwich, not really enjoying it, but more savouring the openness of sky, the light and the green. But before long, the scene perturbed: the Deluxe Cinema that had become a nightclub; the forlorn aura of the museum; the receding presence of the tennis courts where she had learned the game and the huge, silvery expanse of NAPA, like an alien spaceship landed on the shoulder of the savannah. All that cold steel against the living backdrop of green was hard to digest. *Where was it all going?* Perhaps as a remedy to the dead-end she felt she had met, she reminded herself, "Today, you walking the whole thing..." and set off again.

Her step was light in her sandals, and though the wind wrecked her morning's labour with the curling iron, she pressed on, strolling past the college, the stretch with the Seven, pausing to admire the buildings, then stopping to buy a coconut from a vendor she had to wake from his nap on a nearby bench. Perhaps recognising who she was, but not feeling at liberty to say so, he took his time selecting what he judged to be a really good nut and, after gingerly handing it to her, offered a straw and waited for her to peel off the wrapping so that he could discard it himself.

"Careful, eh. Mine the water on yuh clothes," he cautioned, treating her like a tourist.

When she had finished, he received the empty shell with both hands and asked almost shyly, "You is the Minister wife?" He didn't care to wait for confirmation and moved swiftly to his real question, "The bossman doing good? Election coming. I feel it in meh bones."

She let him keep the change from the twenty, felt his eyes linger on her as she walked away.

The Minister's wife. Yes, she needed air. She found a bench

facing the Botanical Gardens. Mostly the years had been good. She couldn't complain. She had taken in her stride all the official functions, the never-ending political rallies, the Old Year's night bash at the PM's residence, the Panorama finals in the VIP box with the other wives. It had all been fine – more than just a manageable life – until the scrutiny started. There were the public accusations of entanglements and missteps, improprieties of all kinds – all judiciously denied – but as the years trickled away, it was more about the two of them, what they had left, or, even more daunting, what they still had to fill the gap between them.

Through the samaan trees and palms, Mavis could see the President's House, the old Governor General's place, now in disrepair.

"Fifty years, next year."

Out of sight, on La Trinity Road, stood a sprawling new construction, a modern palace that was the legacy of the last regime. She focused again on the Victorian style of the President's House. Some political pundits speculated that the new place was really meant to be its sly usurper – for a new time. The bacchanal never ended.

She was with the Minister at the opening the previous year. His party then formed the opposition. A grand zafay was the promise.

"Fancy housewarming," she remembered saying as they prepared to leave home.

The Minister didn't comment. She would not have expected any different. He bad-mouthed no one, at least not in her company. The trouble was that she never knew whether to admire or suspect the staunch discipline he had developed around not speaking to her about his colleagues. Yet she never tired of testing this resolve.

"He certainly spent enough of the people's money on that building."

"One day for Peter; one day for Paul."

That was all. Maybe his reticence was an indication of how

well he understood the things that could happen to a person in high office. She didn't press further and took his maxim to mean that he expected the tables would soon turn. There was talk of it, even then. The party would have its chance. *One day for Peter…*

It was at this point she noticed a slight change in the weather. Clouds had gathered but not enough to present an immediate threat, but after she felt the first cold sting on the back of her hand, she realised she had lost track of time. If she wanted to escape the worst of the approaching rush hour, she had to get moving, maybe even catch a taxi heading out of Cascade or St Ann's. She resumed her walk. With each step, another drop landed, precursors of the surprising gust that swept across the savannah bringing with it much more than a sprinkling.

"How strange!" she thought.

They were her exact words that day of the grand housewarming at La Fantasie Road.

The PM was showing off his new residence to his cabinet, government officials, other dignitaries and friends, when a dog, a hungry stray, trespassed into the well-guarded compound. The commissioned choir was in the middle of its rousing rendition of *Elijah's Day* at the very moment the mongrel decided to risk everything by paddling across the width of the massive swimming pool in the front courtyard, paddling with all his might through the clean, tile-blue water, until he had landed on the other side where the housewarming guests were gathered.

Just as the hymn was about to reach its glorious climax, just before the untimely electricity blackout that brought the proceedings to an abrupt halt, the intruder anchored his four feet and proceeded to violently shake dry his flea-ridden shag in the middle of that distinguished company. She and the Minister, standing in the range of the spray, were well doused.

"What the jail!" he exclaimed and marched out, with her in tow, without saying a word to the host.

"This thing far from over," she had thought as they drove home in a cloud of silence.

"How strange."

The memory kept her walking towards town, following the eastern rim of the savannah past the Belmont Circular Road and Jerningham Avenue. She crossed over to link with Memorial Square, blind to the gridlock of vehicles, their occupants anxious to get out of the city. She walked past Holy Name and the General Hospital. The downpour had begun.

She walked, feeling in her step a rhythm that reached back to the time when the city was home, with streets, shops and people she really knew as she traipsed through in her uniform – and to a time when she had fallen in love.

Approaching Renegades panyard, a realization dawned. So much of life after London and her marriage had passed by in cars, moving from here to there, and missing the life in-between. All that life gone by like a movie she hadn't been watching. She was too busy going elsewhere, to destinations that ended in safe car parks. This city had slipped away from her long ago.

When Mavis found herself abreast of the boys' school that backed Rosary Church, she swung west onto Park Street and found herself at its door on Henry. The building was under renovation and the sexton was about to close for the night, but he let her in. She explained that she wanted to see the original altar. Maybe he recognised her, or felt sorry for her. She was soaked through; she could see that her appearance troubled him.

A web of scaffolding occupied the main church, framing the walls and reaching to the high Gothic ceiling. In the gloom of the building, Mavis felt she was crossing into another time. She moved forward, boarded on either side by a network of pipes. At the front, from the base of the sanctuary, she saw him.

"That dog!" she heard herself exclaim.

The black and white hound, on the very top of the altar's

elaborate back wall, sat attentively at the Holy Mother's feet, with the two saints on either side. It was when she accompanied Great Aunt on her private pilgrimage of churches that she had seen him. St Dominic's dog and *The Hound of Heaven*, woven in her mind during those slow hours when she answered in turn… *Pray for us sinners now and at the hour* … She would wait for the novena booklets and prayer cards, their edges frayed from use, to be solemnly fished from Aunt's huge handbag. Then she was set free to wonder around the church, always quietly, to gaze at the stations hung on the walls and at the altar, where the dog sat happily adoring, she imagined, the somewhat grown Infant on his mother's lap.

At the end came the lighting of the candles: always two.

"One for Mavis and one for…"

The voice was so secret, so shrouded in sad tenderness, she had never fully heard the whispered name, and her asking got lost in the ritual silence that followed.

"One for…?"

Back on the street again, Mavis stood in wonder.

Her mind churned over the puzzle as she made her way down Henry Street. The missing name she had almost forgotten. Whose was it? The rain really started to pour, and with it the growing demand to release her bowels.

"We reach," Maureen announced.

They had turned into a compound where the buildings were lined up and set perpendicular to the street in tacit resistance to its flow. Somewhere from the shadows, a dog pounced first on Maureen and next on Mavis.

"Ok Rex, take it easy!" Maureen protested, trying to contain the animal's excitement. "What kinda behaviour is that? Leave the lady alone. And look at you, soaking wet. Dreevaying again, eh boy?"

She fondly patted his head.

The occupants inside heard the commotion and the door

that faced them swung open. A wholesome smell of soup greeted them, and from within a young man parted an emerald curtain and came forward. He held two toddlers, one in each arm, their heads pillowed on his shoulders. In silhouette, he looked to Mavis like a tree.

"Keeper!" Maureen erupted.

Her joy was unbridled as she ran towards him.

In the background, Mavis heard the boosted pitch of a television advertisement. Her thoughts went to the Minister, his wanting her to listen to his speech.

SISTER, SISTER

Beatrice wasn't into staging unnecessary dramas. She hadn't planned to put one down on the Belmont taxi stand that evening. Not after what had happened at the Broadway intersection, and the loss of the kingfish. *Hustling, always hustling – you busier than the Prime Minister.* That was what Joyce said. What hurt Beatrice was that Ganga would be disappointed. The fish was to celebrate her birthday. Not the one on her birth paper, but the anniversary of the day she had come home to them. Mama had always kept it up.

Mama was gone, rest her soul, but Joyce would be there – the three of them singing at the top of their lungs, *Happy Birthday to you*. No matter how the years piled on, Ganga never stopped flapping her arms and clapping as she sang her version, her *To ME* added with not an ounce of restraint in celebrating her own self. That was the joy she brought them – to see her so elated, her moon-face like a new coin, and running a river that no amount of wiping up could stop. But what really got her going was her favourite song; it beat "London Bridge" and "Brown Girl" hands down, because it was her signal that it was time to go out:

Incy wincy spider climbing up a spout,
Down came the rain and washed the spider out...

Okay, lift the latch and, see, now the gate could open, honey. Very good, Sara. Ganga-Ganga is good-good girl! God-good girl... When we leave out one letter O, see what happen, baby?

> *God-Good-Girl. Say it together A B C D... E F... and what next? G is for Good and G is for who else... God and who else... Yes, baby, Y-E-S...*

No she hadn't planned to play a mas' that evening, but it was an emergency. Joyce had to take up work and she'd promised to get home in good time. How would it will look if the Matron turned up late for work? Well, things could happen. If worse come to worse, Joyce could leave Ganga next door with Teacher. It wasn't ideal because although her heart was gold, Teacher was getting on, and lately her habit was to fall asleep. What else to do? The day had run away on her. Now rain – and curfew on its tail.

The mistake she had made was to overstay at the protest that day. There was noise to make, and Beatrice didn't need encouragement to take up herself and join any march, any strike. Any worthy cause, she was there, out in front with her piece to say. So when the news came about the inexcusable deaths at the Women's Hospital in Mt. Hope, she put down her sewing and started to think about the sign she was going to make, with Ganga right next to her eager to help form the letters. Joyce was home that day so her path was clear.

Those who knew Beatrice best, said it was Ganga who had made her so conscious from young – *political* was the word. And that had nothing to do with waving a flag for any party. Beatrice would tell anybody: *Justice, that is my purpose. Not no flower. Not no sun or whatever symbol they pushing.* Who knows, maybe that is also what Joyce saw and where she had found her own strength. Some said Ganga brought out that part of Joyce, too.

Unwarranted deaths in the nation's hospitals. Ridiculous! She had to do something. "Children are dying!", "Mothers are dying!", "Do Something!" How else to put that fact on the national agenda? She had to do her small part.

Two heads always better than one – that is true. When Beatrice reached parliament that morning, the nation's veteran protester was already on location and turning heads. She wore a body-suit made up to look like a naked newborn. So all Beatrice had to do was contribute her words to complete the mas'. As the day progressed, the protest gained momentum and that caused her to stay longer than she had planned, although there was plenty else on her plate. The fish had to be bought and Joyce had to go to work. Added to that, rain was threatening. Rain. It excited Ganga. Ever since a baby, she had to get in it.

> *... Out came the rain and washed the spider out...*
> *Sara is Incy wincy? That is right, my lady Sara. And Ganga – Sara, too, is me?*

Mama had blamed Beatrice for that confusion, and Joyce took that side. But Beatrice felt she had a case and she never let it go. Ganga was Sara – and Beatrice? Well, Back Lane made things easy. "Sisters", that was how everybody knew them, although there was no blood relation. Sara from day one was everybody's spoiled fish. Later, when Joyce came, she too got the name. Beatrice had taken her in as a tenant after the lady from Rogers Street passed, and the upkeep stopped coming. Seamstress pay wasn't enough to manage the house.

Joyce was a *Pinkie* in training at the General Hospital, from quite Tamana way, and didn't take to the nurses' dorm. Well, from the first time Ganga set eyes on Joyce, she won't let her go, and Joyce wasn't different. It was a match made in heaven, more than they could know. Both of them like peas in a pod, so much so that Beatrice had to find a way to get between those two so she won't lose her place in all that love.

Time passed and Joyce stayed on, occupying the smaller second room even after she was well-qualified and working full time. Beatrice and Sara were in the larger front one that was full of the evening sun. Soon, the three of them were shining like 100 watt bulbs – Beatrice and Ganga, Joyce and Ganga, Beatrice and, in time to come, Matron. Nobody's business but theirs was how the street settled with it. Who would have thought Sara would have two sisters when she had lost one? That may be the case, though sometimes Joyce was known to put her foot down and say all the sisters she ever had were up in Tamana. Well, you know how they say, when it rains it pours.

Incy wincy spider climbing up a spout.
Down came the rain and washed the spider out…

Turn left. Now, we walking to the end of the lane. Turn right. Walk to the traffic lights. See, blue ribbon on the hand is right, and red on the next one is left. Soon-soon we never need them again. Now, what else is red, little lady? Don't forget to wait, wait for the pretty red light… Bea, hold your sister's *hand… Look, look… then cross over. This is the savannah, Missy. Say it with Mama: Red is S-T-O-P. So what is green? … Say it with me. Who is a good-good girl. Now run…*

No she wasn't at all planning to play-ah-mas', not after the day she'd had. Late. Rain, and curfew on its tail; getting home wasn't going to be easy. So when the taxi made its appearance, with the packed pavement of would-be-passengers on high alert for the first chance to jump in, Beatrice knew that the odds were against her. She did the next best thing – she faked a faint. In the middle of the people's street, she went down.

Now people might want to wash their mouth on the country, about how it gone to the dogs, and whatsoever. There may be plenty truth in that – in a certain way. But one thing they can't ever say is that there is no love in the place. People knew when it was time to put away the nonsense and just be human, though sometimes life might have to turn you upside down to bring that single point home.

And that is what they proved when Beatrice dropped down in the road that evening. They forgot their jostle to get into the car and rescued the lady, who they could see was bruised-up already and having a hard time. *Domestic trouble*, somebody whispered, until in the middle of the fray, the realization came that she was one of the regulars who, from time to time, picketed the nation's parliament.

Not everyone agreed with her methods, but she gave them a voice. It was a chance to give back. So they deposited Beatrice like she was royalty in the front seat of the car, with one of passengers at the back fanning her with a copy of *The Focus.* That was how she was able to make her way home, and just in time because it really started to rain.

Incy wincy spider climbing up the spout.
Down came the rain and washed the spider out...

Yes, sugar dumplin, green is GO... This is the savannah. What colour is the grass? Now that is a hard one, Miss Pretty. Come, let both of us think this over... Now run when I say GO... One, two, three... GO, baby, go – that too is Green. O Lord, Beatrice let the chile win, nah. That is advantage. Oh gosh, hold back, girl, both of you could win sometimes. (That was Mama – always full of sense).

*

"*Out came the sun and dried the spider out...*"

That same Saturday, the day Mama brought her home, it had rained whole morning. People said like the place was crying tears for how West Indies went and lose the Test match to England, and big riot erupt. But by two o'clock all grief stopped and the sun was back again. Mama was working then for the Madam on Rogers Street, with the twins. Big secret. Big shame. The mother wasn't good fourteen. Not a word about how that business transpired, but the great aunt ended up with the twins. They say, and this nobody ever proved right or wrong, that the priest and them put a lock on her mouth. Poor thing.

Mama was hanging clothes, mostly sheets and baby things, in-between complaining about the match. She didn't mince matters with her cricket. You could swear she was right there when Charran was judged run out, and ruction in the place.

"Imagine, first Test," she went on, with Beatrice her audience, "and he make a duck! Those boys can't handle England? And they talking Independence in two years? Chut – that is serious business!"

The little transistor radio that was never far from Mama when she was working told the whole thing – how like Bryner later sang, "the Test match turn into a carnival." Not the Doc nor Constantine could stop the Guinness Stand from raining bottles onto the pitch. People didn't believe the call. *Big cheat!*

"Run out," Mama repeated in disbelief. "Those fellas better pull up they socks, and stop putting the place in doubt!"

But more than cricket was on Mama's mind that day, and like her stewing for the loss didn't satisfy, she turned on Beatrice who was sitting on the concrete slab, not too far from the washtub.

"I tired tell you, Bea, to get up from that ground. Yuh womb going to catch cold, girl."

Only nine years old, but long time Beatrice own-way, and maybe that was the blessing she passed onto that day, because she stayed right where she was. Then something told her to turn around. Madam Eleanor was standing by the backdoor, and she was holding the baby like dirty clothes. Maybe, the child wanted changing, but she wasn't able – not with the diaper part, but with the child.

"Too much!" – so she was always complaining, since the births. Mama had a heart big like the globe, that is true, and she felt it for the Madam, who never married, never brought chick nor child into the world, but whatever straw they decided to draw, she was the one left responsible. But that is a tale for another book.

Who would ever think anybody won't want Sara? That bright moon of a face that was all smiles like life itself was joy enough. She daily reminded that happy wasn't a season you had to wait for and it wasn't anybody's permission to give. She was like first scripture – Sara the little princess of the impossible. Who wouldn't want to keep her?

Madam Eleanor.

"Too much. Not one but two, and look at this one – just look at her!"

So she went on like misery that was looking for company.

Yes, the mother had twins, and Ganga was the one that spoiled from inside – that was how the Madam talked. Too long in the passage and on top of that mongoloid – the nasty word she used, although the young mother at least had the presence of mind to say her name was Sara. Poor thing. She didn't last long after the births. And that was how the Madam was left to care for the girls – alone…

Maybe it was the cross she couldn't carry that brought her to the back steps that day. Maybe the rain was what caused the slip as she claimed. But who wouldn't want little Sara? It was like God sent her here just to be happy, like her one mission was to laugh like pebbles pitched over water. But Madam wasn't laughing back. She couldn't take off her worried, twist-up face. She wasn't saying, *Pretty baby*. Or *Who's a good baby?* You know, like normal. But thank God, Sara never needed help in smiling. And that was what she was doing, because Beatrice saw her moon-face plain as day when she turned around and then…

SPLA-TAAU!! Smack inside the washtub, and faster than lightning Beatrice dashed over and snatched her out. God doh sleep. Not a scratch. Look at that. Wet like a fish, licking at the soapsuds and singing her Ganga, Ganga tune. The fact was Ganga loved water. Since that "yard" incident, as it came to be called whenever memory threw it up, that was the case, and she never changed.

Meantime the Madam was busy making her excuse.

"I slipped. That is all. I tired tell you to throw bleach on those steps. As God is my witness, I slipped."

Mama never disagreed. She listened, her face like a judge. After the lady made her case, she quietly packed up her bags. Not a word. That was the last straw. She couldn't work there any more. Not after that. In her best voice she made it plain.

"I will care for this child, Ma'm. Month-end send my pay in what I charge you for my washing. You will have to find a new help with that part."

Jus' so Mama informed her. She didn't blank an eye. The Madam looked like a cross between guilty and relief. Poor soul, she was really seeing trouble. Never mind, Bea and Mama went home with Sara, a bundle that wanted to jump from Mama's arms whenever Beatrice sang, *Ganga, Ganga*. An angel was with that little girl, that day. How else to explain? How else to explain why Ganga loved water so? She had to get in it.

*

...and incy wincy spider went up the spout again.

Sabana is a big-big O. A circle and zero. Not one and two... but running around and around in a circle... then brown girl in a ring... You too bright, Madam Ganga. And what if I say the Savannah look like Mama's elbow? See... now show me yours, Miss Lady...

Don't forget to wipe that nose. Here, I pinning this wash-rag on your dress. See, name and home write there. Now let us go all the way around... Come, Miss Lady, follow the people... We making the big, giant circle... and back home Joycey making ice-cream for Miss Ganga. Come... let us run... Come we walking around. Follow the people, Ganga... we going ... left right, left right... hands in the air ... Left right, left right ... POW! Left right, left right ... POW!

The taxi dropped Beatrice exactly at her door, and the driver refused to take his pay.

"That one on me, Miss Monsegue," he said and drove away.

What to say? People really have heart in this place. But when Beatrice called by Teacher and got no answer, and when she saw that the latch on her gate was drawn back, she seized the situation. Ganga was gone. What to tell Joyce? Only one place to look...

AN APPARITION

Who could tell what really happened? People were huddled under the stores that lined Independence Square from Charlotte to George Streets. Rain. Flood. Transport scarce. Lockdown in One Love country. This-Party-that-Party-tug-a-war. Bailouts. Commissions of Enquiry. Unity. Integrity. Transparency. Talk since Adam was a little boy. People tired listen. Tired complain. But what allyuh worried about? The place blessed – *La Trinity*. No worries. Fete to forget. That self may be the problem or the salvation. People believed everything would fix itself while thief of all description looting the treasury, gangster multiplying like mosquitoes, and the real passport in the place is *who-you-know* until somebody buss yuh pipe and make you serve a little time.

Pundits and seers set up shop at every corner. What this country needs is a father with twenty-twenty vision, a firm-hand and a true prophet batting in the wings. Some disagree. A mother with endless arms of care to put the nation's house in order would do the trick. Was that the malady? That since Columbus, the powers that be never stopped thinking that they were leading a pack of children. All manner of things buzzing in people's heads, like somebody upset a beehive. People were taking *the pain… the bruises* for the love of a place. Maybe the solution was to wait, but even waiting needed a lesson about how to do just that without putting liberty in jail.

So to those stranded on the pavement in Port of Spain, the sight of REDEMPTION ploughing along through the water-logged streets in the steady stream of packed-up vehicles looked like the last chance to get out of the storm before lockdown. Any transport would do the job. People started to flag him down. Terence, seeing that there was so much work, was tempted to stop, but he was headed home. He slid the duffle from the seat to the floor, kept his windows up, and mimed for the street, "I not working". He had to get off the road. Tomorrow, he would square with Marcus and the job would be over. Keeper had dropped the ball.

Who could say what took place? People couldn't make sense of it, but speculation was never in short supply. Maybe a bad hit turned his head and caused him to slam brakes for no reason at all. But Terence was no piper – it wasn't in him. The man cool. Easy. He was never tied up with gang or police. He was not a badjohn. All people could say was that now and then – when the van was working – he would pull a little bull on the weekends, going as far as Carenage or up Belmont, even Laventille way – if he felt it could take the hill. The man had no story to talk about. Maybe that was the giveaway something was brewing. Better to deal direct with a vexed hurricane than a pond that was standing still.

So Terence had no story that anybody could tell. Except if you count the time he buss a man head for calling him Chinee. People call people whatever they want in this place. Terence didn't see it that way.

"That is not my name!" he shouted, like the devil was in his tail.

The fella was out cold with the first blow. Ten stitches to close back his head.

That happened so long ago people hardly remembered this was the same Terence. Monday or Sunday – no change. What people could say? Only that for years he rented a room at the back of Hung Lee's grocery nobody had ever seen. He was working there, too, bagging, packing and delivering goods. Some claimed the man had money in the bank. How else he could afford to buy a van? Not only that. Put gas in the tank and keep it on the road? Every spare moment, he was tinkering in the engine, doing all the fixing. And he had Ragga adding gadgets and lights for friend-pay, like he was driving a plane.

If anybody wanted to tell a story about Terence, they would have to make one up. Like the candle some claimed he was holding for Maureen, but she blanked him outright for Keeper since school days. People liked to talk, so they concluded that was why he floored the fella for not using his proper name. But you know how story could grow young. Like the talk that Terence was the son Hung Lee had on the side with Janice, the one cashier who never got fired since he opened the business. Truth be told, Terence looked a little that way. But who's to tell?

Who felt they knew better would say Terence had a jumbie that he never took the time to settle with. Watch him! Like the way he liked to take the backseat. Playing spectator was only mongoose tactics. But until the happening by the Cathedral on the day of the storm nobody saw him that way – and that was still only half the tale.

That evening, Terence was on his way home after dropping off a fella he had picked up by French Street on the Tragarete Road side. He didn't know the man, but he looked like he had just finished whatever was his work, and was trying to get home. When they had passed the Treasury, out of the blue, the man belt out, "Stop!" and jumped out, hurry-hurry, never mind rain was falling bucket a drop.

How *exactly* Terence make jail was a story he alone could explain; part of the story came from the prison chaplain who Terence put his confidence in, and another piece from someone who was family to the prison officer who heard the whole conversation direct, although he wasn't supposed to be listening. Who to believe? Anything called *confidential* in this place is evening news headlines.

Anyway, the priest who did the listening was young. Everything about him was new-new – the shoes, the black dress pants and shirt, the Roman collar white like a Colgate smile. But ole talk aside, he wasn't no joke priest. He could make a big man hit the floor when he opened his mouth to pray his prayers. Serious business! They say he get that gift. And jail, the story went, was where the Lord chose to put Terence down so he could raise him up again. So Terence started to talk.

REDEMPTION was cruising along Independence Square. His usual route was to turn up Duncan so he could find a park on the eastern end of Queen Street. He was waving his "No" to anybody who tried to flag him down. He was travelling easy on account of the water in the road and the police that were making their rounds, cracking down on crime, lights flashing so people won't get it in their heads to loiter. But who would have anything in mind other than getting out of the rain and into a house that was dry?

Yes, he was heading east. That is what anybody could claim to have seen in the moments before the blackout – and plenty claim to have seen the whole thing. When the van reached neck and neck with the Cathedral, it came to a halt – no signal. The car behind had to swerve to avoid running into his backside. Tail-ended might be the proper word. "Get away! Yes, Fadda, by ah hair!"

As soon as people realize that is stop he stop, they made a dash for the van, hoping to get in. Maybe the man had changed his mind about not working. No such luck! When they got to the vehicle, every door was locked.

"Yuh taking passenger or not, driver? People want to go home."

Terence sat behind the wheel and stared at the road like he was in a trance, his arms in the air like when police shout "hands-up!" Nothing doing. The man freeze.

In the meantime, traffic was backing-up past where Cipriani stood overlooking everything, weeping much more than with the rain. The lawmen came, torchlights flashing, and put an end to the whole thing. Terence was a statue in the driver's seat. That was when the story get real bright. The first part was easy – police wanted him to explain the duffle bag. Weed fuh-so. And on top of that, gun. Imagine that! Terence turn runner. Who would believe that? The law had ways and means. People not dotish. That, though, could be idle talk. Who would want to frame the man? The Force might have a few bad apples; that is how things go, but plenty just out to do their work – protect and serve. The fact of the matter is – never put yuh head on a block for anybody. Imagine, Terence – hold that!

The story making the rounds, running like caraili over every fence. The mystery was why the man stopped at all. He coulda get away. Some things have no way to explain. Not that people had any quarrel that the law did its job. Yuh make your bed, yuh lie in it. But jail was calling the man that day.

So the story go. Terence was minding his own business, going home. He had come neck and neck with the Cathedral when, jus' so, somebody appeared in the middle of the road in full white robe. He slammed the brakes.

"What the hell…!"

Quick-quick he crossed himself, though he had forgotten the order and Holy Spirit came in first. Not that it matter. He could see plain that the man was His Grace, decked off as usual in his official priest clothes like he was born so.

"Now, I doh claim to be a praying man," Terence told the chaplain. "Church see me for funeral and wedding. Yuh understand."

The priest nodded and crossed his legs, to signal he was in for the long haul.

"An apparition, a ghost, a spirit – am I hearing you correctly?"

"In the middle of the road in all that rain, the man appear, and he dry like he inside his house. And, priest, up to now, I cyah believe it! The man call me by name."

The chaplain nodded again, took a break from his listening pose to swirl his wristwatch so he could see its face. A nice watch too. Big brand – anybody could see the man liked *nice*. He was a work in progress, like everybody else. What mattered was that he was listening to the brother.

"A man like His Grace know my name," Terence continued. "He look me straight in the eye. *Terence*, he say, *what foolishness yuh get yuhself in*?"

"Padre, I not lying, but the man talk like we is long time friend."

"And this man you saw was in fact the Archbishop? Am I correct?"

"Yes. I went to the funeral. Well, I was on the Promenade when they put him down, and when the bell start to ring, I not shame to say, Priest, I cry tears. And I never know him personal."

"And what, on the occasion you are speaking about, brother, did His Grace actually say to you that brought about the change you claim?"

"I not sure what, but when he call my name, I realise my rope run out. I say, *Terence, what yuh doing? This is not you.*"

"And what happened next?"

"Next? Nothing. The man say, *Exactly, son*, like he read my mind, and he sign the cross and, BAM – he gone!"

"And then?"

"Well, I find myself kneeling down in the road saying prayers I could hardly remember. But I tell you this, Padre, mark my words: the man is a saint."

That was how Terence put the matter. And who's to say different?

CURFEW RUN

7.45 p.m. Curfew Friday. The highway is free, though the now light rain makes the surface appear glassy. Curepe Junction, Valsayn, Gran Bazaar fly by. Adesh approaches the old Aranguez intersection and steps down hard, opening up the Hilux.

The vehicle is five years old, but you couldn't tell. It didn't have much road time – low mileage and an immaculate interior. It is his first long run. St Augustine to Wrightson Road, north along Colville, across Ariapita and Tragarete, up the Boulevard, around the savannah, over Lady Young to join the highway again and home well before nine. Simple. No stops. His personal challenge: make it back to base with time to spare. He relaxes into the push. Sweet. No regrets.

It was a great buy. The woman wanted a quick sale.

"Too much crime. Time for a change."

She was emigrating. Maybe she felt lucky to be leaving. He didn't care. Life was good for him, but he could tell she wanted to say more about where she was going. It was important to her – to make him feel left behind.

"Toronto," she said. " I have a brother over there. Things getting too ridiculous. Look at that mess with the insurance company. Big tief but the law can't seem to touch them! Now this..."

She never named the "this." He remembered nodding his agreement, but only because her decision had created an opportunity for him. The pick-up truck was a steal. Everything was exactly as she had stated in the newspaper. No accidents. No loan payments. No defects. Perfect.

"Yes, time for a change."

"Good luck with that," he had said, not really meaning it. He was really the lucky one.

He leans towards the mirror, flashes himself a winning smile, realizes he is not strapped in and quickly reaches for the belt.

Things were always like that with him. Easy. Born in a lucky cycle, the pundit gave him the name Adesh at the reading his grandmother had insisted on, although it was no longer his mother's faith. Joash was what the Pastor at the Calvary Hill Tabernacle baptized him, the result of a solemn cutting of the Bible by the praying ladies. That was the word they brought for Sumintra, the story of a good king turned bad and punished for his offences. But no one ever called him by that name. The pundit's choice had somehow remained and his grandmother went to her grave with that one satisfaction – her faith had won.

Adesh bore allegiance to no God. Three words – *Thank you Jesus* – had carved up his mother's life between her cashier's job at the mini-mart and church. Home was a pit-stop. It was a world he felt grow tighter around his neck with every passing year. When things went well – *Thank you Jesus.* When times were hard – *Thank you Jeeeeesus.* When there was need and nothing seemed to be happening – *Thank you J-eeeee-SUS*. He wanted nothing to do with the God she insisted was the only father he needed in this world. He didn't want her cross – whatever it was.

The pundit had gotten one thing right. The stars were indeed well aligned at his birth. The same luck that brought him the Hilux had helped him seal the lab job on the campus. He loved what he did, gathering evidence, testing, ensuring that the facts were accurately recorded and the conclusions objectively drawn. No bluffing. No grey. Only saying what *is* on a particular day. The security of the immediate relaxed and reassured him. No guessing.

Driving was the same. Any road led him from point A to

point B. No big mystery. He loved making a carefully mapped-out route, calculating the time, and, when necessary, manoeuvring a network of back streets to avoid traffic. Barring the unpredictable – probabilities he easily accommodated – one could get to any destination one wanted once the way to get there was known. It was a simple enough creed.

Landscape sweeps by faster than thought – DHL, Courts, Lifestyle, swamp land on the west. He caresses the wheel, listens to the swish of the tires on the wet road. He glances back at the tray. Empty. With weight she would really sit on the road.

On the Beetham stretch he clocks 140km and feels the engine daring him to tip into overdrive. The Sunny comes back in a flash. Nippy and good-looking. Black. Silver rims and mean low profiles. A finger automatically traces the scar on his forehead. He would miss the old ride, but the pick-up is by far a better buy. He double-checks his seat belt. 94.1 starts to jam Lil Wayne. *Now you in the corner tryna put it together / How to love, how to love*. He ups the volume, rocks back and listens, but notes the bass doesn't have enough kick.

The truck rushes through the usual haze that hangs over the district, like a permanent blight.

"Pure poison. People dying by the second," he thinks.

He holds to what has become a single white line down the middle of the highway. The cluster of houses built so low to the ground that they seem stamped upon disappear in a blink. Blue lights flashing in the distance, heading east, draw his attention. He relaxes the accelerator to be safe. A patrol car zooms by, busy about its own business. He feeds the engine again.

Overdrive kicks in. Lil Wayne is really rocking so he tips to max... *See you had a lot of crooks try to steal your heart / Never really had luck, couldn't ever figure out / How to love*.

His watch beeps. 8 o'clock. Suddenly the city's lights go out. He does not see it coming. Worse. He isn't even sure what he sees. The figure, but a shadow, dashes across the road at Sealots. He isn't sure. Only the awful blunt thud and double bump as the vehicle weaves then pushes forward.

"What the..."

Astonishment or fear settles like a boulder in his stomach. He stops, puts down the window and looks back. The road is a blank. The whole city is in darkness. Sensation does somersaults. He imagines something has landed in the tray. He glances back. Nothing. It is too dark.

"Relax," he tells himself. "Maybe a dog."

He hopes there is no damage to the vehicle, but doesn't want to linger. The district isn't safe. One last look before he jams the accelerator to the floor. As the Hilux speeds off, he wonders if what he sees descending from the night sky is a mix raindrops and engine exhaust.

The thought is still with him when he's forced to brake hard a second time. The tray careens but he somehow manages to regain control.

Roadblock.

An officer draped in a black raincoat signals with his torchlight for him to put down his window. Another flashes his light in the cabin and moves away to examine the tray.

"You in a hurry, brother?"

The speaker is hidden behind the beam of his torchlight, which travels to the passenger seat.

"You late for something?" he asks, refocusing his light on Adesh's face.

Adesh makes a move to shield his eyes but decides against it.

"Just hustling to beat the curfew, officer," he answers.

"Oh-ho. Licence and insurance..."

He is reviewing the documents when an officer calls from the back.

"Sarge!"

"Yeah."

"Yuh not going to believe what we have here."

The sergeant signals to another officer to take his place and disappears.

"Well, well..." he says on his return, smiling broadly.

"Sir, step out of the vehicle, nice and slow."

Adesh complies. Light rain stings his face.

"What is your name, sir?"

"Adesh Subir. I didn't mean to speed, officer... Curfew. I was..."

"This is your vehicle... ah, Mr. Subir?"

The officer re-examines the driver's permit. Adesh realizes his error.

"Joash, officer," he adds quickly. "Adesh is a home name."

The sergeant ignores the correction.

"So tell me, Mr. Joash Subir, are you carrying fish tonight?"

"What? Me?"

"Doh play dotish. Yuh hear what I say."

"Tell me, what is your trade?" the sergeant asks and breaks into a mischievous grin.

An officer steps forward. Two hefty sharks are slapped onto the wet asphalt. In the light that is trained on them, their open eyes seem amazingly alive.

Adesh shakes his head.

"Not mine, officer."

"Sure, brother."

"Not mine," he protests again.

"And..." the sergeant continues, "explain this?"

The officer stoops and extracts a cylindrical package wrapped in cellophane from the gut of a fish.

"What is that, Mr Subir?"

Adesh drops to his knees.

"What is this – time for prayers? I don't have all night," the sergeant jeers.

The officers are all smiles.

Adesh looks directly into the light and bellows, "Na-Na!"

Some said they heard that cry as far as Moruga.

BLACKOUT

When ole talk start to spread about the Port of Spain blackout, the blame was put on what had happened to Prince. Strands of his severed hair had somehow entangled the main generators at Power Gen. The pundit's dream was roped in as confirmation. Somebody made the connection and it caught on.

And if that wasn't enough, a member of the environmentalists group camped outside the PM's residence – to protest the highway that would destroy the swamplands – contributed another strand to the matter: Papa Bois and Mama D'glo had donated some of theirs to the cause – and they had Mama's comb as proof to silence detractors. Contrary to concerns that this tale would undermine the legitimacy of the protest, it only served to strengthen it. The story started to stretch like laglee. Now everybody – the Carib Queen from Arima, and wherever the rest had first come from – African, Indian, Chinee, Syrian, Venezuelan, small island, French Creole – tout moun, jumped in to add their piece. A movement had formed, and Prince was the beginning.

'Nancy story or not, the fact was that the whole Gulf, and quite down to Columbus Channel in the south, was covered with a massive net of seaweed, that the experts at Environmental Affairs, in the service of rationality and national calm, identified as sargassum. Climate change was the problem. All up the islands was no different. Even Tobago had to announce a crisis despite the harm the admission would do to tourism. But seaweed or not, people had enough common sense to know when more was in the mortar than the pestle. No one, not even the experts, could explain how in just a few hours, for miles and miles, all you could see was weed.

Another set of people was of the opinion that they should never have disturbed the dragon on top the Red House, sea serpent or not. Why take it down? That was what started the whole thing – foolishness in high places and too much superstition. But talk wasn't satisfied with that. The problem was all the gossip about Mother Lutchmi running the country. Whoever heard of that! A fella who became a born-again even pledged never to eat another doubles again. Religion and all turned pappy-show. What about that church hidden away in the bush they say taxpayers were paying for? Anybody was worried about that? No. Something more was happening. Something more was needed. But what?

Fishermen, alarmed by the effects of the sargassum on their livelihood, contacted *Friends of the Sea*. Word of their meeting reached the Minister of Land, Sea and Food Planning via an informant he had hired, out of his own pocket, to keep him in the loop and one-step ahead of the game. It was his first stint in politics and he had his eyes on a larger prize down the road. So seeing the chance to gain some points, he lost no time.

An official statement was released. The population should look on the bright side. The seaweed was nature's gift of free fertilizer and animal food. The situation was not to be lamented. Nevertheless, a clean-up was already in the pipeline, pending parliamentary approval. As far as he was concerned – but this was off-the-record – dissatisfied tourists who lodged complaints on international travel advisories about the state of Tobago's beaches (as if Trinidad didn't matter), would just have to settle for freshwater or choose other destinations. Tourism was not a GDP staple.

The Minister of All Things Legal happened to be in the waiting room of the television station, preparing for his national address, when his colleague's statement was aired. He was disappointed. The man, bowtie or not, should have had more sense than that. Yet he understood how at this level newcomers could easily go astray, say foolish things. He knew this all too well. The last thing the nation needed was a bogus pick-me-up like his colleague had just offered. He would certainly make no mention of it in his speech. Cheap optimism was beyond him. What he would offer was a gesture of good faith, evidence of living up to the government's commitment to transparency and accountability. Getting tangled up in seaweed was not his priority. He needed to defend the road the state had chosen, and the country needed to hear a promise of brighter days.

Meanwhile the PM was in the air, or had already landed in New York to lobby for global disarmament at the UN. Smart. Photogenic. She could dress. What else to say? Unprecedented. For the very first time, it wasn't about suits and ties. So what to say? When the PM returned she would do her part before the nation's cameras. That she was doing the maternal thing, showing care, would be an unfair assessment. Yes, a language had to be found to deal with the new circumstances. He made a note of it. She meant well – a fighter – but there were flaws some felt could be too easily exploited. Someone had to watch her back. That was his role – a small part to play in the service of the bigger picture. The stakes were enormous.

Truth be told, the Minister was under plenty stress. Too many things were in play. Peeved policyholders were venting about the insurance fraud. The Police Commissioner imported from foreign seemed preoccupied with flying planes. The trade unions were not cooperating. Too many botched deliveries were being reported at the nation's hospitals. Gunmen were out of control. Drugs. Journalists and columnists were taking liberties with facts that implicated his esteemed office in wrongdoings. Emailgate. Section 34. The failure of the EMA. One of the country's brightest on a sixty-day hunger strike. The situation was volatile. The man was billed to die. And now this weed substance that was growing a mile a minute in the Gulf, and, if he understood correctly, had allegedly infiltrated the residence of the PM. Overload.

Scandal after scandal. He was fed-up, but he had a job to do that night. The whole country was waiting. He had been carefully prepped by the technical team at the studio, and was now seated, shoulders square, his face powdered, fitted with the microphone and ready to go in FIVE, FOUR, THREE, TWO... He was ready. The way was clear. The moment was all his... ONE...

His beginning was strong: "Good night, my fellow citizens. Tonight, I am here to assure you that the government you elected to root out corruption and incompetence, to root out nepotism and nemacarism is in control..."

Then – jus' so. Blackout.

In the darkened studio he wondered where the problem lay – with him or the nation's generators. Maybe the SUV's 360 spin had unbalanced him more than he realised. But his health was good. He had always been careful. Power-walks every morning, his weights workout, his regimen of natural juices and, to complete it, deep breathing. The formula had never failed him.

Instinctively he reached for his wrist. The calm concentration of his sister's face, so much like their mother's, came to him as she tied the red and yellow sacred threads.

With every passing year her devotion to the rituals of their childhood tugged at him. All her degrees and travel, the big house and even the loss of the daughter snatched away and never found, had not pulled her away. The certitude of their faith brought him back to his beginnings. When the rituals were over, when the mantras grew distant and the smell of the sandalwood faded, he felt adrift but for the memory of their devotion, and if that was faith, perhaps he too believed. It was enough for him but not for Mavis.

He remembered her look that morning when she realised he had gone for prayers. She never hid the fact that she thought his devotions fraudulent. His "little superstition", as she called it, of running to the pundit whenever things were rough. She had long distanced herself from religion and allowed the children to choose when they were good and ready.

He hadn't interfered, but held to his line that his religious observances were not her business. Like his job, it was a world he had chosen to keep her from entering. It was much too precious. He was well aware of the restlessness that signalled her doubts about his position – and what he felt was her habit of listening for the slightest hint of rejection in every word he spoke. That was her struggle, not his. She needed to face her own demons in that department.

No the problem could not be with him. The day had gone as planned but for the messy business with that woman, Sumintra alias Judith. She had interrupted his carefully organized schedule. From the first he had known she wanted something – delivery of some *favour* from long ago. She was clearly disturbed. In her black pumps, accordion-pleated navy-blue skirt and white blouse, she looked like a delayed schoolgirl. Yes, he remembered her. No use denying that; but she had not aged well. *Sorrowing* was how he would describe her – a plain and tight-lipped woman who had put herself on the shelf. He had to exercise enormous restraint to keep listening as she dug up foolishness from his greenhorn days in politics. Yes, mistakes had been made, but she could have chosen a better day to offload her bad conscience about this son she claimed was his.

The surprise was that apart from getting him to acknowledge the deed and the end product, she wanted nothing. No money. No strings pulled. Nothing but to let him know that the young man in the photograph was the child he fathered, more than twenty years ago. It was a past he'd all but forgotten. Others had made worse errors. The woman must be mad stirring up such nonsense. No use denying there was something familiar about the young man in the photograph. Something about the square forehead and trademark tuft of grey and the dimpled chin. He reached for the spot like someone looking in a mirror.

"Jesus! No joke."

It was but a whispered acknowledgement before he caved into his chair.

"Exactly!"

That was all she had said. What he saw as she turned and walked away was a woman swinging her tail. Yes, swinging her tail, happy as pappy.

"You hold that!" he imagined he heard her say.

The next thing he knew someone had thrust a light to his face. Someone else was feeding him sips of water that smelt of too much chlorine.

"Yuh pass out, Mr. Minister," a voice counselled from the jumbled shadow of heads.

"Blackout," said another. "The generators going to kick in jus' now."

Maybe the information was meant as an assurance that the nation was safely in the dark about what had transpired with him. What about his speech? He had a message for the country.

"Hush allyuh! He trying to say something."

The shadows huddled closer.

"C-c-aul Ma-bis..."

"What he say?"

"N-AW... Ma-a- ma-buf... "

"What? Ma-ma... Is his mother he calling?"

"Doh talk chupidness. Listen to the man."

"Maa-BIFF... MA-bif."

The realisation came.

"Oh shit! Stroke."

A KILLING

Three things unnerve Marcus about his line of work. The first is making eye contact with his targets and seeing their quick slide from surprise to terror, and that glimpse of disbelief bordering on a plea. The second is the stink of hot metal and burnt sulphur that clings to his clothes. The third he can barely admit because there is nothing tangible he can assign to the need that wells up in him to pray, beseeching the same mercy he denies his kills.

Together they make a bittersweet cocktail that triggers an explosion in his veins, an exhilaration that blends defeated fear with a charge of absolute abandon, a power that lifts him out of himself until the release comes – an awful freedom bursting like some trapped beast from his skin. Each kill is the drug that does it, releases him from himself – even if temporarily.

But afterwards, and just before, the only remedy he can find to still his desired and feared annihilation is to immerse himself in water, wherever he finds it: a standpipe, a shower, a river, the sea. Water. It soothes, washes him. His is that kind of occupation. Blood. The antidote is purification. More than anything he wants to be free.

Everything has been perfectly timed. The only unforeseen circumstance is the rain, but it works for him, like an unexpected washing. He waits at his lookout point at the far end of the street, his face up-tilted, allowing the drops to bathe him as he rehearses the kill. His jobs are always clean. No struggle. No mess-ups that need correction. In. BAM. Out. So from the moment the car swings onto the street, he readies himself, gets the pedals of his freestyle in push-off position.

The vehicle slows, veering ever so slightly to ride the sleeping policeman – his signal to move, cruising forward, watching for the anticipated braking to negotiate the second hump, the stop, directly under the street light. The iron wheels of the automatic gate begin their rumble along the tracks, background music to the scene and his cue to speed up, getting just near enough. His target is almost too simple. She likes the windows down, no matter the heat. She is that kind of woman – in love with her climate, wanting to feel the air, the ground, hear the sounds, smell the streets.

Once or twice he has watched her during her Saturday morning jogs. He enjoys studying his targets, learning their habits. He knows that she is not light on her feet but that her short, steady stride chips away at the miles. Dark sunglasses – the wraparound type he too likes – worn for more than the glare, he felt. She is known – her views, her picture are always in the newspapers. The life that has chosen her also exposes her; privacy, he thinks, was what she craves – the reason for the shades.

He remembers the half-grimace on her face as she runs, as if movement is a decision of will against shutdown, a determination to keep pushing towards some invisible place where there is not just a finish line, but a purpose that demands her complete presence. That drive has made her somebody's problem – the one who ordered the job.

The lawyer-lady is different. People appreciate her. No nonsense lady. But she says too much and knows too much. There are battles she should leave alone. Doors she should not open. Not her. She has more than stepped on somebody's corn, so she has to go. Something is wrong with that. Sad. He feels he understands that push to get beyond herself. The difference is that he really wants to escape himself.

The bottom line – he has a job to deliver. No questions. People will weep for years when he takes her down. He, too, is sorry, but cannot stop the wheels. He clenches and releases his left fist, grimacing at an imagined or remembered pain. It is a reflex he has never lost from that long ago time... *playing man*, is all his mother has ever said about his rumoured escapades... *only playing man*. Her helplessness still angers him.

His plan is to fire one shot directly to the head, no need to stop, just glide by, and then pump to the foreshore, fly across the highway and down past the mall into the sea. Abandon the bike, dunk the gun and swim – just swim to wherever the current takes him.

The car stops at the gate. At about twenty feet from the vehicle, he veers right, and uses his foot to brake. An impulsive change of plan he cannot explain. Time slows. He feels he is looking at a movie frame by frame. Through raindrops that seem as long as needles, he lifts his arm. The gun is in place targeting the lady. One flow. Now they are face to face, but only he can be seen. He prepares to squeeze. In spite of the headlights, he knows exactly where to fix his aim. Head first. And just so, the lights dip. The wipers keep working. Each swipe casual, unhurried. She wants him to see her. Maybe he, too, wants to be seen.

There is no fear in her eyes. Instead, he feels she really sees him. She is that kind of lady. One second... two... three... Unexpectedly, a head appears on the passenger's side, the face drawn close to the windscreen. Marcus hesitates... Why is he there? His eyes are all he sees – opened wide. His face. There is no mistaking what he reads. Wonder and fear interchange, leaving only an unspoken word that is not the child's but his... *Mercy, Marcus.* Not in the plan. He looks again. Now there is no one but the lady. He cannot turn back.

The streetlights go off. BLACKOUT. He squeezes like a reflex, relieved to be freed from those eyes that held him, if only for a few seconds, in an embrace that whispered the question, *Why?* The need to empty his gun, like his very life depends on it, consumes him. He fires again and again into the darkness. He cannot stop shooting as though driven not just to empty himself of the death he has come to deliver, but is its very name.

In that split second before all the lights go out, the lady gives him a look he can't forget. What of the boy – was he in there? All is one flow. She wants nothing for herself. The *why* he read there, in a flash, is really his question. He knows, in that moment of her wordless asking about the Marcus beyond and before the kill, she is the kind that can never stay in a grave. She is the kind that cannot die – the only reason they wanted her dead. Too alive!

He fires. God is on his lips, but without sweetness. It is now too late to apologise – and to whom? He wants to let loose his rage and disappointment and shame, not as an excuse for himself, or as any justification for taking revenge or destroying another life, but as a cry to be free, to give somebody the death he can no longer carry. It is not him, the Marcus beyond, but an imposter that outruns him. So he fires until the last unresponsive click of the trigger is the emptiness he too feels. No fear or anguish or regret or imagined sorrow. Nothing.

The lawyer-lady, in a split second, tells him, in the intimacy of the darkness, that she can carry even the beast in him. "Is alright. Take a five, Marcus. Take five," he hears her say through the awful agony of the face she allows him to meet. No judgement, just that solemn invitation. Does he imagine it? "Take five." But even that generosity cannot stir in him the will to be again simply Marcus, freed of any cause for what he has become. What about the boy? He cannot remember who that was.

Someone from a neighbouring house lets loose a dog. He sees the light of a torch at a window. Time to ride. He shifts into action, shoves off and does not look back. That too is his weapon.

Crossing the highway is easy. Raindrops and tears mingle. He pumps the pedals hard, feeling the burn in his thigh muscles and calves, pumping too so that the breeze takes away the smell of burnt sulphur. What is it? The breath of a volcano? Rotten eggs? The exhaust of Hell? Sweat trickles down his face and back. Rain. Sweat. Tears. His heart is racing ahead of him. Sweat. Rain. Tears. He pumps so hard he feels his legs will give out. His thoughts catch him on the stretch.

The lady's eyes were asking him *Why*, like an offer of a life, a call to possess the Marcus behind the mask – this gunman, gangster, the mas' that has already killed him. He has to free himself. Take responsibility. *For what? Everything? Yuh playing mas' and 'fraid powder? Take five, she says.* He pumps like his life depends on each push towards that face she mirrored for him, even in the death he came to deliver. And what about that little boy? Was he even there... the Marcus that disappeared? And he is back to that scene, after so many years.

The room is cramped with furniture. Miss Atkins, old as the hills, smells of Bengay and soft candle. A glossy picture of Jesus with heart exposed is overhead... He does not want to be back there. He thinks instead of his legs. He imagines the growth of wings somewhere at his ankles, or maybe they would burst from his thighs. One more hard push on the pedal – lift-off. He feels it coming, hovering on the tip. He remembers when Amber tried to remind him about Charlo's birthday, he'd spat into the phone, "Fuck him." Not really meaning it. He blames him for nothing. Wants nothing from him. Not any more. Who he has become has no one point of blame, only beginnings that grew into a colossal dark. The Marcus after... what?

One more push. He lifts himself off the saddle, pedal-sprinting. His backside is in the air, torso over the handlebars that he grips like a choke, his elbows bent, his legs pumping hard... He remembers the snickering at the window, the bedsprings, the muffled struggle beneath the pressed-down pillow. He hears weeping, but he keeps pumping, only pretending for the faces at the window, as God is his judge, telling the woman, "Shut up!" She won't hear to just keep quiet.

Only fifteen – they should never have made him do it. Not

that; but he agrees, wanting more of what he thought was theirs to give – a chance to belong to something. Poor Miss Atkins. Not wanting to see her face, he holds the pillow there, only pretending, but she wouldn't stop bawling, her fingers clawing at his back, and the smell of urine and everything old stifling him.

He smells the sea. Rotting seaweed. Sulphur. Almost there. He feels the rise approaching, the release to air, and with it the flood of terror and pleasure, the stretch of power and surrender. Free. He isn't going to stop. He rides and rides, ramps the seawall. Levitation. Tide is high. He breaks surface through a mat of seaweed. A thousand fingers tear at him and his plunge down is an eternal *why* – the lawyer-lady's question. And that boy – was he ever there? He should not have been there. Choked laughter pursues his plummet into what he hopes is an answer.

Poor Miss Atkins – older than his mother. He is in tears. Almost done, home free and somehow his bowels let loose. Just so, like a judgment on himself, he sits in his own waste. Those faces at the window… and Miss Atkins is on the bed, clutching the nightdress and sobbing with her face to the wall, her knees in her chest. Over her head is that longhaired Jesus, illuminated, smooth, a kind of distant calm, looking down at him, and pointing to a naked heart… He sees her face, again, the lawyer-lady's; she never judged him, her eyes, like the picture's over the bed, asking him *why* – the offer of a life, to possess the Marcus behind the killer that was playing him.

Marcus after… He never let them forget that madman he had become, and how much they should fear and hate him. No mercy. Her sobbing stops after the lash that knocks her cold. The laughter, no more… In that void, he feels the floor open and swallow him; but he finds his feet and pelts through the rain, holding the fractured fist, his eyes a blank stare at the unrelenting dark. Hell. He has been there and never came back. That is what they fear.

The blow is hard. Something like old iron when he hits the

bottom, but the nothingness that comes is a long release as his body buoys up to surface from what seems an incredible deep, breaking through the thick carpet of weed. Upheld. For the first time free to sleep, really sleep. Marcus beyond the deed – finally.

A DECISION

"SoE bring the luck."

That was what the depot concluded when Lucky stopped to make his boast that the land was finally sold.

"So yuh turn real estate agent in tru'?"

"What kinda question is *dat*? What yuh mean if I selling property?"

He could have spoken to the wind. The loud slam of the draughts ended wherever that talk was going. It was Friday evening and curfew was coming. Beers and rum were passing. Cards and draughts were playing. Friday and lockdown was closing in. What is that? The country had really gone to the worse. More than a little vexation resounded when a man lost his king or got his jack hung. Not only words could talk.

The sting in his leg told Lucky a truth about himself since the accident, and one he couldn't shake – about a name that was his but was stolen away. Lucky was the self he had been left with. He headed for his van like a man looking for a hiding place, wondering why that fish was grinning at him.

Craig they called him. No nickname, because he was so much himself – maybe too much himself. There was no half or quarter name the village could reduce him to – the way they called George, *Bait*, Fletcher, *Mistake*, Wilfred, *Guts* and Pierre, *Shortcut*. He was just Craig. Nothing about him was deficient. Complete. Some would say beautiful – like sunshine when the clouds stepped aside, or polished like sea-washed stone.

It wasn't hard for people to love him. They wanted to hear what he had to say. They wanted to be close – as if life itself issued from his presence. Craig was sweet, a sweetness that women fought each other to keep. When he walked the road like its owner, his tallness lifted all who saw him. He made them wonder what stock he had come from before longtime memory closed its door. Mandingo. Yoruba. Ibo. Ashanti. They didn't know exactly who had made the journey, but he made them think with pride of ancestors and a landscape they never knew.

And whoever wanted to stake their claim to Spanish, or whatever mix, they found their temptation to boast melt like salt in rain if Craig happened to pass that way. The island, though, was his only claim, if you really talked to him. He wasn't going back and he wasn't looking to go anywhere. When people talked about "migrate", he sucked his teeth and walked away. It was enough, the island that had made him the "all" the coast saw and loved deeper than he had fathomed. He was their "over there" and "right here" wrapped up in one.

The weird thing about that day was he didn't go out with the boat as usual. Something inside told him, *Craig, stay home.* And that was what he did. So when the boats came in that evening, he went down to the jetty to help offload the catch, not working too hard, just supporting and listening to the stories the men had come back with, and dropping in a word here and there. Then, just so, like a piece of bad-mind take it, the shark everybody thought was well dead suddenly convulsed and, in a split second, swung its head up and around, snapping at the first thing in its way – Craig's calf – then flung itself back into the sea.

"No lie! Jus' so –"

That Friday, all the way to Grande hospital in the tray of Bait's pick-up, Lucky's head rolled in Aura's lap. He wouldn't stop mumbling that he had seen it coming.

"See what? What he see?"

"I know that fish had me in mind... Stay home, Craig, it say. I coming to meet you today."

Nobody could make sense of what he was saying. The only

explanation was that his head was going wild on account of all the blood he was losing. Blood trailed behind the whole road to Grande. Not even the sun could shine. It remained hide-up behind a cloud that wouldn't even rain – like when grief is long past tears. More stitches than he could count to close the wound.

When they let him go home, Craig was a different man. Vexed with nothing but his own self, because that shark went away with his flesh. That is how people, if they really spoke their mind, would describe him. Since that day he realised that life was bigger than his command. That was what owned his anger. He'd been thrown from the sky. He was no longer walking on clouds and holding court with the sun and stars. A gift to the whole damn place – that was Craig. And then, jus-so, he found himself limping through the world with a pain that wouldn't go.

There was a loss he wanted to recover. He left the depot with the bitter taste of the fellas' refusal to accept the new face he had shown them, denying him even the change he was trying so hard to make. But as the starter bounced and he moved into gear, for the very first time he could give a clear name to the pain. The loss had stolen away the self he loved – maybe a little too much – and wanted back. His whole life since the accident had been a long wail. It was time for all that water to stop. Time to stop the life from leaking out of him. He needed to find that shark.

Nobody saw him but the sea that lapped the jetty. He had doubled back, and with the curfew coming, the whole place was locked up for the night. He positioned himself to board the very pirogue he had sold to Guts for half its worth when he'd decided against making a life on the coast. With his right foot set in place to hold the craft steady, he angled himself to let his good leg take the weight, and cautiously let himself down.

The fall was hard – straight back, his bottom on the floor of the boat, both legs in the air, his arms splayed out like a capsized spider. Blackout. He must have been out for a good minute, but before his mind could convince him that should turn back, he scrambled to his feet, ignoring the warm trickle of blood down the back of his neck. Telling himself that he was no stranger to the water, he secured the oars, one at a time, each in its lock. That was easy. Next, he untied the mooring rope.

No big plan. He was going to row out to the deep and anchor inside the headlands, just far enough to drop a decent line. That fish would be waiting for him, like the day it did its mischief. He wanted an answer. Why out of all the people on that jetty had it chosen to mash-up his life? His calf muscle twitched, ready to throw a tantrum and his sense of betrayal returned over how the fellas had shot down the hard work he was doing in the real estate business. They wanted to deny him his own anger. Imagine that! They felt that *he* owed them something. What? An explanation, an apology? His living was his own damn business to choose.

But Craig had never put down his side of the story long enough to find out the hurt he had caused them. What they saw was a bleeding dissatisfaction with the card life had dealt him, and not only that. The very sea that put bread on all their tables was what he despised and spat on because he couldn't forgive her bad side. He couldn't love the *all* that she gave. It became the unspoken rift between them – the prolonged vexness at his loss and the incompleteness he carried about as though he was other than of the human race, or that he alone knew suffering.

"Is you and me, fish. Tonight is my turn to wait."

His fingers found the wound at the back of his neck.

"Blood draw again. Yuh hear me? Is time we finish this…"

The anchor plunged to the bottom. He watched like a man in a dream as the rope followed its weight into the deep. When he felt the drift of the vessel had ceased, he cut in half the small tuna he'd found by the depot, washed the blood in the sea and threaded the halves to a single hook. It was all the bait he had.

Not ideal, but if that fish was out there, looking for him, bait didn't matter. He flung the line into the darkness – no overhead spin – just the strength of his arm. When the plunk came he waited a little then reeled in the slack. A cross swell caused the boat to do a double wobble and he grabbed hold of the sides, not wanting another slip.

"I waiting on you, fish," he shouted into the darkness. "We have business to finish."

The first raindrop smacked Lucky's forehead. He took his first real glance at the shore. One or two heavy clouds had gathered, stealing the moonlight, and the mountains, blanketed in night, companioned the craggy coastline where, like a necklace unevenly strung with gems, lights from the houses shone. He thought of Aura. She would be worried, but he didn't want to risk her changing his mind. His time had come to face the dark that was eating away at his insides. He switched off his phone.

All his restlessness and questioning seemed like infantile rants in the face of the land that lay hushed in mystery. Stillness enveloped him, a quiet that was of the place, especially at night when the only moving body was the sea, with its constant arrival of waves. That unbridled liveliness was the measure that kept faith with the far off, but always approaching day. He had forgotten what the land looked like from the sea, the exhilaration that always came with the prospect of reaching harbour and reconnecting with the solidity of the earth beneath his feet. He had forgotten the gratitude he felt at that welcome. A rush of regret enveloped him for the sea and coast he had so foolishly deserted.

The drizzle grew steadier. He looked towards the darkened horizon, but could tell that the bad weather was coming off the land. Usually the big rains came to the coast *off* the sea. It was probably raining heavily inland and the clouds were spreading out north to the coast. He wondered about the lawyer-lady, whether she had made it home okay. She had promised to call.

"Probably ole talk," he told himself.

Raindrops started pelting down like pebbles.

He reached into the storage cabin under the bow and pulled out two tarpaulin raincoats – yellow. Not a colour the coast wanted to see these days – too much bad politics. He let the party association slide as the flags of the river-feasts down Salybia came to mind. They always drew his attention and, although he wasn't a believer, he had gathered enough about their colours to know what some meant. Like the red of Shango. He wondered at the yellow..."

The sky opened and he made haste to pull on the better of the two raincoats, then slid way down into the belly of the boat, the weightless nylon resting lightly on his index finger, ready to alert him to the slightest tug. There was nothing to worry about. He was still near enough to the shore to look like the boat was anchored. If the coastguard happened to pass, they wouldn't take him on. He was out of sight. Water slapped and sucked at the boat, rocking him until his body anticipated the flow. A calm he had almost forgotten the ocean could give took hold of him.

Time rolled by. All he had was the drift of his thoughts and his calf, throbbing – that absent piece of himself talking and talking, on and on, in a dull elongated drone, like a note released underwater. He never noticed when sleep nuzzled close and hugged him up like a lover. He never felt the first strong tug on the line. He never felt the desperate yank that pulled and pulled him through the night...

CHARLO'S DAY

"The las' time I check, this is a free country," Charlo insisted. "And I..." he thumped his chest, "...have money to pay..." He dipped into his pants' pocket, drew out a wad of blue bills and fanned them out on the bar like a deck of cards.

A few men seated at the tables closest to the door stood up to get a better view.

"My own sweat and blood!" he concluded.

"*Dat* is de man!"

Charlo smiled. Whole day he had been on a drinking spree, moving from bar to bar making one announcement.

"Beers for everybody. I buying."

No one bothered to raise a question about the occasion. He was buying and that was enough – generosity or folly, it didn't matter. He made good his offer. Rounds flowed freely for anybody to claim a drink. The slaps of gratitude on his back and the odd man shaking his hand kept him from pausing to acknowledge the lump in his throat and the heaviness in his chest.

There was still no word from Amber. His hope was that they could have lunch, just the two of them. Marcus was a wall. It was a waste of time trying to connect. She'd said she was working, but would see what was possible. All he wanted was an hour – to celebrate a little. At least he could share a meal with his daughter. That would help. The bitterness of his chance meeting with Marcus that week in Port of Spain lingered. He was in line at the Sando taxi stand waiting for passengers.

"Still driving taxi for people?"

The voice came from behind him. Charlo could hear the sulky boy behind the grownup words, but the comment connected like a blow. He turned to face this son, who had become even more of a stranger in the garb of his new faith.

"At least I make my money honest," he retorted. "Not what I hear people saying 'bout you."

The laughter that spilled from Marcus was pure scorn, but Charlo sensed that this son still loved him enough to want his rejection to hurt.

"Is honest money," Charlo repeated.

In spite of everything, he hoped that what people said about Marcus was just gossip, that the boy hadn't turned out rotten. His son despised him. Charlo could understand that. He was the one who had walked out to follow a bogus dream in New York. People made mistakes. Hard as he tried, he could not muster a different response to close the gap between them. Every meeting increased his need to disown the Marcus he couldn't engage. The boy followed his own mind. He wasn't responsible for that. He couldn't be blamed for what Marcus chose to make of his life.

That day Charlo felt he wanted to do something big with the money he had earned, no matter what Marcus thought of him. As long as the rounds of drinks kept going, he remained one step ahead of the meeting he knew he had to have with his pain. Now this bartender wanted to put an end his spree.

"I see yuh holding big notes, pardner, but I have to close. That is the law now."

Seecharan raised his voice at the last sentence. Business was slow since the curfew, but he and Vindra were ready to settle for the smaller takings as a price for the promise the government had made for change. The place would be different. Bandit had too much freedom – every day was a kidnap or a killing. His own brother had to find a million dollars he didn't have to get back his own son. Things would change. He glanced nervously at the dingy curtain behind him. It blocked customers from seeing into the storeroom that also doubled as a downstairs kitchen when the shop was open. Vindra, he knew, was there, seated on the old wicker chair, hearing everything.

Charlo fixed his eyes on the bartender.

"I have money," he repeated, daring him to feast again on the spectacle of notes. "I am a paying customer. It have people here I order drinks for."

But when he turned around to face the said *people*, his elbows gripping the counter for balance, only a regular they called Thirsty lingered, nursing an almost empty beer bottle, no doubt hoping for a freebee for the road.

"Man, I have to obey the law. Is time for me to close. Like yuh want me mek a jail?"

Charlo wanted confrontation not a surrender. He didn't budge.

Vindra decided it was time to make an appearance. She drew aside the curtain and stood in the doorway holding a phone against her very pregnant belly.

"Uncle, yuh want we call po-lice nah?"

Seecharan stood frozen, not even nodding in support of his wife's threat. The men held each other's gaze in the heavy silence. Thirsty, sensing that it was time to give up the ghost, quickly gobbled the remainder of his beer, saluted the air and staggered into the night.

"Look, we open again tomorrow. We ain't want no trouble, bassman," Seecharan pleaded.

No one expected what followed. Tears flooded Charlo's face.

Seecharan found the eyes of an equally surprised Vindra. A strange kind of tenderness for the fella washed over him, but all he could offer as a response was to repeat, "We closing now, bredder."

As unannounced as his tears, Charlo's fists came crashing down on the counter.

"I thirsty, Indian. Bring a STAG!"

Seecharan knew better than to protest. He went to the freezer, at the same time signalling to his wife to back off. A bottle that was already opened and frothing at the mouth was put before Charlo.

"Hold yuh money, man." His tone was now considerably softened.

Charlo sensed the man was offering some kind of apology. He too wanted to say sorry, but something stronger than that need made him gather up his money, with the exception of a single blue bill.

"Keep the change."

He took a long swig, spilling beer on himself as he drank. It was all the power he felt he had – to make them wait. He brought the empty bottle down on the counter with a loud blow, then headed for the door.

"Tomorrow, Uncle," Seecharan offered good-naturedly.

"I doh give a rat's arse 'bout tomorrow!"

Charlo took a long look at the heavy sky and allowed a few drops to wet his face. He regretted disrespecting the man. He only wanted to spend his money, to give back something on his birthday.

Sando was a ghost town. All the bars were closed, the vendors gone home. The wet streets glistened under the streetlights. He looked at his cellphone. Amber's missed text showed up. She couldn't make it tomorrow – "Busy".

One more glance at the message box and he drifted in the direction of High Street. Eight-fifty. Hunger bit at him but everywhere was closed up for the night. Even KFC. He slumped to the edge of the wet pavement, his back to the Colonel.

"Not even a damn star tonight," he complained as he looked up at the blank sky.

The dizzying rotation of blue lights intruded. The officer on the passenger side exited the vehicle. He was dressed in civilian clothes, like his partner at the wheel.

"Curfew in effect in ten minutes. You aware of that?"

Charlo propped himself up on his elbows.

"I know, officer, but I feel like I want to be outside tonight. I not troubling nobody. You see me interfering with anybody?"

"Like we have a badjohn here, Calvin. It look like he had a few."

"We have no time with this, Neil. Get him moving. Where he living?"

A door opened and closed. The other officer leaned casually against the SUV, offering his presence more as a signal for his partner to wrap things up than give any assistance.

The grip on Charlo's upper arm was rough as the officer named Neil forced him to his feet. He tried to stop the feeling that the pavement was in motion by plunging his hands in his pockets.

"What happen, the floor wining?" the officer taunted. A firm clout to the back of his head threw Charlo against the vehicle.

"Yuh is a beast or what. Why yuh treating me so?"

"Back-chatting an officer of the law is serious business."

"Nobody own my mouth."

The second blow was to his left kidney.

"It have a curfew. Yuh brain dead or what? Where yuh living?"

Calvin felt it was time to step in. "Neil's aggression was unwarranted and time was wasting.

"You hear the officer. Answer the question. We giving you a break tonight."

"Yuh backside is where I living!"

Officer Neil increased the force on Charlo's jacked arm. Anticipating another punch, he took a deep breath and threw his full weight back against the officer and bellowed like a battle cry, "Fuck de curfew! Today, Mathias Charles Valentine celebrating his birthday!"

In the scuffle that lasted for what seemed only a second, Charlo was firmly pinned to the pavement.

"Well, well, it must be my lucky day. That make it three," Neil said. "Breaking curfew, resisting arrest and using obscene language in the presence of an officer of the LAW."

Calvin was taken by something else.

"What you say your name is? Valentine? Is Valentine?"

"Yuh damn right. Mathias Charles..."

A rush of perspiration dampened Calvin's face.

"Amber... that is your daughter?"

"What the hell that is to you?"

"Leave the man alone, Neil. He just tight."

"But he..."

"I say leave him alone!"

Neil complied; the name his partner had spoken rang a bell.

Calvin stormed back to the jeep and slammed the door shut.

"Is your lucky day, ole' timer. Go home or tonight is jail."

From the cold concrete Charlo could see the old Colonel looking on and smiling contentedly, long after the flashing blue had vanished.

AURA'S NEWS

When Aura didn't get word from Lucky, she called Brenda, Shortcut's lady who had taken over the parlour at the depot. She didn't have more to say than he had left the coast long ago. He should be close to home, so don't worry. The weakness that dropped on her told Aura different. Something was going on. He wasn't answering his phone. Not a soul was on the road except lawmen and hardheaded criminal. So why he wasn't home?

Tears came. She had missed her chance to give him her news that morning. She was sure he would come straight back when he was finished with the sale, so she had held her tongue. The time wasn't right. Let him have his chance to sell the land. She knew the man. Since he decided to pack up and leave the coast, he moved in a cloud she didn't want to trouble. It was better to give him time. The coast was sure to call again. To besides, the plot was still there. Her father had insisted that she took the gift, fending off the enthusiasm of Joyce and Wilfred to relieve her of it, since she was already married and in house.

"Land doh rotten," he had said. "When time come you will know what it waiting there for."

Yes, the land was there, but Lucky had rented the small piece they lived on.

"I have the option to buy," he had told her. "In a few years we could payoff for it."

He had wanted to make his own start, bit by bit. Since the accident, she saw he needed to take charge and feel he was building something. He and the fellas put down the concrete foundation; the walls were only board, but the roof was new, good-grade galvanize. It was home. Aura wasn't a woman to complain, although she had her mind set on better. Work with how life turned each new page. A lesson she had learnt from her mother. "Wait for life to show the hand it want to play. Doh fight and push yuh way. Watch and wait."

Watch. That was how she ended up in the back of Bait's pick-up, holding Craig's head in her lap. Some hand bigger than herself gave her that card to play that day. She had dropped everything she was doing. Fish stopped frying; who wanted cigarettes or plastic bags would have to go elsewhere. Shop closed. Dennis, who she was watching for Cheryl, she snatched from the makeshift playpen behind the counter and put him in her mother's arms. All the way, something was telling her that this was it. Craig wasn't going to die. Her life was going to change. Through thick or thin, even with all that blood in the tray, that day was a beginning.

Aura only smiled at those who felt it was their calling to run they mouth like standpipe and pronounce her a walkover. She told herself, "Wait. Sun and rain shine on toute bagai." Craig was everybody's sweetheart. So she knew it had sour grapes in what they had to say. More than that, he had no special eye for Aura. She wasn't no looker, but she was the one he chose and that hurt them – though some say it was only when he get bruk-up good and proper he settled for her. That was their story. She knew different. Something had passed between them on the road to Grande and *it* had chosen them.

She had her faith: *Wait*. Running to church or behind anybody who claimed to have a calling wasn't her habit. Not since the freshness Deacon Pierre tried on her that harvest day he drank too much plum wine. Her mother laughed it off, saying the man was only joking. Since then – and she was only thirteen – church stopped seeing her. Not her way. She had one creed – *Wait* – and it was the reason she didn't give her news as she watched Lucky, this man born to be by the sea, getting ready to meet the lawyer-lady who wanted to see the property he was trying to sell for the company.

Wait. Nothing to say as she watched him put on his good dress pants, though it was bush he was going to show. She watched him trying to decide between the sky-blue and the white long-sleeve cotton shirts he reserved for weddings and funerals. In the end he pulled the blue one over his new merino. She watched him with his hair trimmed close to the skull, the barber's mark still fresh, the clean rag on his shoulder to wipe away sweat, and the black tall-tops waiting by the kitchen door, shiny clean. He was ready to go, looking official. No more buss-up short pants and dingy T-shirt or vest like he used to wear in the depot, his skin and hair smelling of sun and sea. She watched him drive away in the same van, but now with *Life-Style Properties* branded on the doors.

Nine p.m. – curfew time. No van pulled into the yard. No dogs going wild until they heard the familiar whistle that triggered their ecstatic whining. Lucky home. Aura, too, smiling inside, and asking, "Yuh hungry?" but not waiting for the "yes" she knew was coming. She dished out whatever she had cooked that day, big portions of everything, though he complained he couldn't eat all that she had piled on his plate. Lucky home. A joy she never stopped feeling, even after he took them from the coast, away from her family and friends. Far from the light and the breeze she knew as morning, the smell of cocoa-tea and roast bakes that were her evenings. But she wasn't afraid to ask her question: "Boy, yuh know what yuh doing?" And although he would not answer, and *that* she understood, all she would tell herself was that she could wait. She never loved nobody so.

Not every change is for better. Sometimes a change is the very thing that needs changing. That was how Aura saw Lucky's leaving for La Horquetta – a place she had to memorize how to spell. That was where they ended-up, living in a sweatbox behind all that wrought-iron, but she was bearing up, though her life had boiled down to four rooms and a small piece of yard paved over with solid concrete. "No problems with weeds," the owner had boasted. But when twelve o'clock sun beat down on the place, Aura swore she was baking in hell-self. Whole day, two fans blowing, and nothing green near except what she managed to plant in a few paint pans.

Aura held her peace, but thinking all the time of the plot up the coast that was waiting for them to make a return. In that cell of a living room, with the curtains tied back to catch whatever little breeze was passing, she felt more and more what it meant to be *outside* – the word the coast used for any place that was not there. Belonging wasn't like a flag or a birth certificate or a passport. It wasn't even a whole island, but the texture of a place – the way warm sea sand felt underfoot and how rain played on a roof. It was the timbre of voices passing by, where, without seeing a single face, each had a name. Yes, they had found themselves *outside*. More and more that absence connected to the absence of the children she always wanted. In the meantime, she'd been determined to find a way to make life grow.

That is when the idea came to start selling snacks, cold drinks and newspapers from inside the small porch that was already burglar-proofed like a cage. People would come to buy. The house had a good position on a corner-lot by the settlement's main road, where the maxis plied for passengers. Sales would be good. Lucky agreed and the owner didn't complain when he put up a sign on the gate that said: *Aura's Parlour*. They were good tenants – quiet, clean, no trouble with the rent. One by one sales came as the word spread. Aura was glad to keep busy, although it never left her mind that they were living a bogus change. Lucky had his pain, and she didn't question that.

"I tried. That place treat me like a mango seed it spit out. They giving me a six for a nine every time they take out the boat. One minute they say the fish not biting. The next minute the engine break down. They robbing me blind, Aura. Nothing there for me," he had complained.

"Those boys know you love the sea," she said. "So maybe it hurt them that you decide never to go out again. Maybe they feel you walk out on them. That ever cross yuh mind, Lucky? That is a love you reject that include them?"

But the man had his mind set, ignoring all the objections that came his way.

"Where yuh going? Yuh born and grow up here."

Those questions tired ask. No matter how they told him life outside not nice, he didn't want to hear.

"We doh have bandit. Where yuh going for some ass with a bad head to shoot you dead?"

Aura knew those men. Rough. She had grown up in that depot where she fried jacks and kingfish slices, kneaded flour for the bakes to put them in. They didn't have much to say unless it was ole talk and picong sharing. The words that made their hearts swell to burst were hard to let go. Maybe they were offering a challenge, but didn't have the words to layout the terms. Lucky didn't want to see that maybe the fellas were trying to say something they couldn't quite express.

People had stopped what they were doing to watch them leave. Cheryl flagged down the van as it passed the Anglican school so Dennis could give her a kiss – now a big boy in third standard. The last one was still in hand.

"We go talk," Cheryl shouted as the van pulled away. "Walk good."

Aura didn't have the voice to make a reply, so she just waved.

Lucky was leaving the sea, but the sea was in him. *That* truth stayed with her through days with nothing in sight but concrete walls and the radio for company. Her creed: the sea will come back to him. She was certain. The tru-tru part of a person never changed. The coast was also in her and was awaiting her deeper "yes." She had been working her way to it – the long-ago invitation Cheryl had made her to attend the feast down by Salybia.

"Jus' come. Look and see what happening."

Aura had only laughed and folded her arms.

"God in everybody," she had pronounced, feeling wise and a little better than her friend, who needed that community of prayers to keep her strong. "Everyday I make *my* prayers. I good. I done with church."

"Come and see, Aura."

She wouldn't budge no matter how Cheryl coaxed.

Aura had been praying for a baby that wouldn't come. After years of obeying all the doctors ordered: no baby. All kinda tests, tablets and tonics. Checking the moon and her temperature, even buying boxers for Lucky to wear. Still no baby. So when the heaviness of La Horquetta started to weigh on her, she decided the time had come to take up Cheryl's invitation to meet her at the next feast. So telling Lucky they were going for a lime, not wanting to risk dissuasion, or to blight with too much talk the blessing she was hoping to get, she found herself in Grande waiting for a transport.

When the maxi reached the Salybia bridge, people had already gathered on the area of beach close to the river's mouth. Devotees were dressed in an array of colours. There was pink, golden yellow, white, blue, red, green and some wore plaids. She didn't know the colour of the feast. Nothing was certain. The gold drew her attention, maybe because of the Ella Andall CD Cheryl had given her for a birthday present one year. A few worshippers held uplifted cocoyea brooms. Even from the road, Aura could hear the drums, the chac-chacs and the choruses: *Yeye Osun, Talade Osun*. It was a new world to her – and maybe that was okay, and she wondered why.

She was late, and with no sign of Cheryl she didn't know what to do with herself, but felt it best to ease her way into the gathering. A few people made her out and nodded their recognition. One or two hugged her and asked how things were going in Arima. She had to find her own feet on that ground, in the flow of the prayers and songs that she didn't really know, but didn't seem strange to her. The altar of offerings on the sand was arranged with every fruit she could name, and cakes and bread; and there were shells and jewellery, coins, bottles of oil and rich, golden honey.

But there was no time for talk because the orisa had come and the babalawo followed her into the water. As the music intensified, the blowing of the conch shell, the drums and the chac-chacs opened a joy of recognition she didn't feel it was right to deny. So she'd joined in the clapping, moving her feet, her body turning side to side with the worshippers on the beach, with the trees on one side and the sea on the other. The full and steady flow of the river carried to the ocean the flowers and pumpkins, melons and figs that were people's prayers for whatever blessings they were hoping to receive.

She never knew how she got there, but she found herself by the side of the river, close to everything, singing the chorus she had picked up – "Osun me ba ibeji lo..." – not knowing what the words meant, but that did not matter. What was greater was the welcome that was opening in her. After the honey libation and a few people had gone into the water as the orisa called them, Cheryl slipped in beside her.

"So yuh come."

"Yes, I here. Present and accounted for," she replied, wanting to make light of being there.

Next thing, the people around were gesturing to Aura.

"Look, she calling you."

"Who, me?"

She looked disbelievingly at the woman the orisa had chosen to ride, thickset as the hills, but bouncing playfully in the river, and waving her to come in."

"Go on, " Cheryl nudged. "Is you she want. Go. Is okay."

"Not in all my clothes, Cheryl!" Aura protested.

Cheryl gave her an encouraging push forward. Aura didn't know how, but her feet had decided before her head and said their own *yes*. The chanting climbed like an agreement the gathering shared. Next thing she was in the water. No explaining how that happened. Only that when that first hug took hold of her, rocked her and lifted her up and bounced her up and down, and put so much laughter in her, she would tell anybody that *that* was the exact moment her womb healed.

After, when Cheryl put the towel over her shoulders and asked how she was feeling, all she could say was, "Happy. Girl, I so happy right now!"

That was August. As October came to its end, she had news she was waiting to tell Lucky.

AMBER'S POEM

on the brink of injured hope / with the pelican flown / comes a heart unfurled / an uplift in lengthening shadow / a light switched on / in rooms empty of reason / an upended bowl / outpouring/an umbrella in rain/canopy of sun/a benediction / in eye-water season/there it comes/a colour christening/the city's red page / a level for *irradiant* highs / it arrives, a note / pitched above a street's downbeat –

Out of the blue the words had started to come. Maybe she had read them somewhere, bits of them, at least. Maybe some were hers. She wasn't a poet – just an ear. The flow was so full she could no longer hear the television's babble. The words had a mission like the rain that beat down on the roof nonstop. No sense in writing anything down. She had lost her notebook somewhere in Scholar's storm – jus' so, jus' so...

Amber had been seated at the security station, rereading what the Minsh had to say about the Music-lady's funeral. She'd made her exit the very day before the SoE was announced – like she had gotten wind of its coming and packed up her soulcase as if to say, "I not in that! All talk done. I gone!"

Now in the night that hung over the city, Amber heard a note walk in on her, not even bothering to knock, like how a melody teased out on a far tenor enters a space...

/ beauty of shell / dot of joy / erupting in all that bring-down / healing amber of undead stone / inverted bulb / of tear / there it comes / to a household in lockdown / long time locked in /

fête singing / No, No we eh going home / to the guns of UN/ just response / jamming down wombs / bandits of dreams / one army too many / rivers of ohoooo missions / nightmare reruns / but here it is / YELLOW / …

And hers wasn't any *silly-season*, vote-fuh-me, party colour. It wasn't an election show wooing votes… She was back again on South Quay that evening, after Cummings had sent her home.

"Resurrection colour."

She'd turned to see who had spoken, talking, she supposed, about the dance the umbrella was doing above the junction. Leant up against the jewellery shop was the same fella with the backpack who had helped cart Scholar away. After the bacchanal was over, when he had returned to collect the bag, she had asked, wanting to tease him, "Boy, like yuh carrying the world on yuh back."

He didn't respond, but his smile, she remembered, was pure sunshine in all that bad weather.

"Ragga is the name," he had said, and was gone.

"Amber," she had responded, but was caught up by the miracle of his word.

"Resurrection."

Highlighted in her mind was a single image from the newspaper article she'd been reading at work: a yellow flower on the Music-lady's casket, keeping company with her trademark cowbell – a farewell in the colour that came home with her after Cuba – La Virgen de Caridad, Havana's patron. What did it mean – this marriage of faiths that had delivered its own eulogy during the silence she had requested? No permission needed. Did anybody hear it? Amber hadn't been there. Never where life was happening, living second-hand.

Yuh head too much in book. Life not on a page. That had been Charlo's teaser to get her to talk whenever he came to check up on she and Marcus. Amber would have nothing to say; she just clasped tighter to whatever book she happened to be reading as she sat on the porch, with the wrought-iron table and a vase of plastic flowers between them. Balanced on the edge would be two boxes of chicken and chips, growing cold, a neglected offering.

They never ate when he was there, preferring to deny him even the small pleasure of seeing them enjoy the treat. She at least sat through his visits. Not Marcus. He escaped to the yard to pelt pebbles at the wall or kill lizards with his slingshot. Whenever her father came by, her mother would find herself by a neighbour, usually Miss Lucy, conveniently caught up in ole talk.

Amber had wanted to go to the Music-lady's funeral. Like everybody else in the place, she felt something big had happened, like when the Head Bishop had passed away – a loss that belonged to everyone, like the day they buried Bradley and the newspaperman, the one the madman had called Smithy – though she'd pretended she didn't know what he was talking about. With only a few minutes to close-up time it was easier to make him just another madman.

She wanted to leave the turnaround space she was renting in the Estate, right under the foot of the Hill – the navel string of every pan note ever played, no matter where the band came from. Panorama and the Music-lady – it didn't matter what your camp was – it was one thing. Even her own mother, Suzanne, with all her complaints – the sugar, the belly, joint-pain and migraine – had found herself in the church by the savannah to pay her respects, as she did to everybody who made the Carnival live – mas' man, musician, calypsonian, whoever – she was there to give her thanks for them and whatever they gave to the only season that called her from the tomb of grief and bad-mind she lived in.

At Carnival-time Suzanne was in the panyard every night the band was practising, wearing the red cap she reserved special for the season, so dew wouldn't settle on her head. She would come back home to report the progress made, the changes, and her judgment about who was and wasn't pulling their weight in the band. "If they doh win this year is because they tief!" After each competition, she returned to the panyard with the players, listening to the postmortems, putting in her two-piece in the quarrels. She was a flame burning with love and danger, anger and praise, sorrow and hope in those days.

Whenever Amber went with her, she saw a new woman. Her support for the band was absolute, like a love determined to remain through thick or thin. Against any badmouth, any disappointment, her mother was there. Not only when they won. Amongst the smell of corn soup and souse, bake and shark, the beers and rum passing hands, and weed sweetening the air, her mother was there, listening, supporting every step towards the day, the eve of Panorama, when the iron rang out from the engine room... ping... ping... ping... and the band burst into perfect song.

Su—zanne! Amber heard afresh the wonderment of the yard when the music caught hold of her mother and she leggo in front of everybody, her backside rolling like nobody's business, for the yard to see and delight in the tribute and benediction she was offering the players. That was the mother Amber, too, looked at with admiration, the woman that the drums brought alive and caused her to put aside the mourning and discontent she carried whole year like a bogus mas'. *SU-zanne!* The woman who talked how each pan put in its say, until the agreement they made was a harmony of the difference each brought to the depth and range.

The truth was Amber, too, wanted to leggo, but there were weights on her feet, a heaviness that had grown on that veranda when Charlo made his sometime visits. Each year, she sat there, not accepting his gift of chicken and chips, she had taken on more and more her mother's bitterness. Nor would she dance when the band held out its hand to her. She couldn't make a fitting response, one that she really wanted to give – to release herself and hear somebody say: *AM-ber! That is you girl!* She couldn't find it in herself to give the response that was hers alone to give. So she stopped going to the yard.

But the feeling that she owed the place something was the reason she had wanted to make her farewell when the pan-lady passed. It was a start. She wanted to say sorry for not answering the drums and letting them walk her through...

a door to opening sound / saving cross of roads / motion of turn / arc of line / to promise of circle / and full pot / libation of sweetness / balm for any shape of hurt / charmer of steel / music-Lady / House of star / and bright skydancer / play NOW / the Sanctus / slow

A knocking at the door woke her, like the beginning or end of the words that filled her from wherever they had come. She had fallen asleep and missed the Minister's speech. The television screen was blank and the electronic clock on the kitchen-counter told her that the electricity supply had been interrupted. It was already well after nine.

"Must be Calvin," she thought.

It was his usual time whenever he worked late and happened to be in the city. She didn't think twice before she opened the door, but had to pull back, more surprised than scared.

"How you find..."

The fella from the Scholar fiasco stood like a wet-fowl in the rain, the knapsack still on his back and a Guinness bottle in his hand.

"Doh frighten," he said, seeing her frown and thinking she was going to either scream or slam the door in his face.

He stepped away and stooped down in the yard to show her she was safe.

"Doh 'fraid. I was in the maxi behind yours and I see where you drop-off."

"Yuh mean you follow me here?" she asked in disbelief, beginning to wonder whether he had been hanging around the place.

"No-no. I not in any foolishness. I was going South..."

He hesitated. She saw his open face. He wanted to gain her confidence and was searching for an approach.

"That is a long story, Miss Amber. I see where you stop. That is all."

He brought the neck of his T-shirt up to his face and wiped it dry.

"Well, what you doing in front my door this time of night?"

Twisting so that one knee was anchored on the ground, he dragged off the backpack and placed it next to the bottle. She saw it was unopened.

"You remember what you ask me?"

He searched her face.

Amber was puzzled. Her inclination was to go back inside and lock the door. Maybe he was in some kind of trouble that it was better to stay far from.

"Ask yuh what?"

"…Miss Amber, I know yuh don't know me from Adam. And for that yuh have a right to close your door, but I feel it in me I could talk to you. That is why I here. And I need to talk to somebody… or I going to mash up this place."

"So why me? Yuh doh have family, a friend somewhere?"

He didn't respond to that question, but gestured at the sodden knapsack.

"Yuh ask me if is the world I have in this bag. Remember?"

So Amber, finding it in herself to answer his call, his voice a solid six bass, moved her body over the threshold like a prisoner leaving her cell and, under the little eave over the front door, she made a seat of the brick she used to keep it open when she wanted a little breeze.

"Ok, Mr. Ragga, tell me yuh story."

NEW LAND

"Blood alone don't make a mother or a father."

That was how Ragga began, sitting on his haunches, refusing, at first, Amber's offer to take shelter under the little eave over the door.

"That was Prince – family when I needed one."

There was no front wall, so he squatted in the middle of the walkway taking the rain. He lifted his head to hold her gaze in the half-light that streamed from the doorway. Amber sensed that a current too deep to break surface stirred beneath the calm she saw there. That exposure, a face sheened with rain, was perhaps the only offering he could make to let her know that she had nothing to fear.

"Yuh understand what I mean?"

The night was a huge hat that canopied him. Beneath the blurred streetlights and watery sky he looked like he belonged to the sea. She folded her arms under her breasts and could only nod as she tried to stay anchored.

She didn't know the man and felt the need to hold back from running ahead of herself, but when he'd smiled at her at the door of *The Focus*, she'd felt a drop in her belly, like the world was falling away. Now he was in her yard, this stranger who had already, in a way, broken into her.

"Yuh doh make me out?" he asked, interrupting her musing. "Plenty times I see you in town, passing in yuh uniform."

"Who, me?"

"No scene. I just around. Yuh always buying papers outside the bank."

His gaze was intent but gentle.

"Yuh like to read..."

"And you like to mine people business," she retorted, but kept her voice soft.

"I have two eyes."

Ragga smiled that morning smile.

She extended her arm so that the water running off the eave beat into her open palm. *The man could talk*, she thought.

He adjusted the position of the knapsack until it sat on the walkway like a meeting point between them.

"So what yuh have in there?" she asked.

Sensing the invitation to relax, he rose and moved closer.

"The reason I wanted to talk to *The Focus* today."

He positioned himself on the edge of the piece of concrete flooring that served as a porch, the still unopened bottle cupped in his hand.

"Prince doh drink rum, but Guinness – he love that more than water."

She allowed him his diversion. Whatever road he wanted his story to travel, she was sure he meant no harm.

"That is how I first know him. Fifty cents, my pay every time he send me to buy a black bottle for him. He use to hustle his transport outside Nagib. *Jus tell them is for Prince*. That was my passport, and I so fas' he start calling me *Toes*."

Amber observed his nod of self-acknowledgment.

"I could run. My real name is Quacey."

"Quacey?"

The question leapt from her. He didn't miss a beat.

"Ragga is what the block name me," he said, hearing her confusion. "It doh mean nothing. Jus' a joke the fellas have on me."

"Well, you have more name than the President!"

They burst out laughing.

She rose and disappeared through the door. The towel she offered Ragga on her return he accepted, but didn't use, choosing instead to hang it around his neck. The rain was a baptism he didn't want to wipe away.

"Prince was home to me. Outside the hardware, I had a life that was bigger than in that room. In there, I see more stars than I could count light-up and die-out with one pull. Puff. Gone."

Amber wasn't sure where he was going, but she was content to follow.

"You know where I learn to read?"

"Where?"

"What school couldn't teach me, I learn from Prince. He driving and I reading for him. *Learn to read and give change and this world can't beat you down.* That was his anthem. The Doc teach him that, he say. I know fellas who hardly know who the Doc is... Yuh could imagine that?"

A convoy of army trucks with a police escort, sirens bawling, swept along the Priority. Ragga sucked his teeth at the scene, then dropped his head between his arms. The sirens trailed away and, as if their disappearance was a signal to surface, he raised his head.

"I doh have no party colour in my blood, not like Prince, but all this chupidness going on is a bad movie if yuh ask me. Only small man they taking down. Even gunman need to get hire. So where the kingpins in all this mess?"

Someone passing in the road, either ignoring the curfew or late getting in, struck a match and the end of a cigarette glowed. Amber saw Ragga's head sink again.

"Girl, this story cyah tell... Sometimes home is a place yuh have to run from to find a home. Yuh understand?"

Amber looked towards the Hill and remembered that she owed her mother a visit. There was, too, Charlo and the birthday lunch she had avoided. And Marcus. She felt the words she needed to say building in her veins like a volcano waiting to explode. Marcus, her twin, he was more than her blood. So how to start that conversation with what he had become, the shadow that none of them could face?

"Yuh ever see a woman twist and turn like a snake because she can't get the hit she crave?"

The question startled Amber.

"What yuh mean, like a piper?"

"My mother."

She didn't know what to say. She had no words for the darkness he had brought to light, and she knew why. She had never had a conversation with her own.

"Nothing perfect," she said. It was all she could manage.

"Blood alone doh make mother or father, and Prince was both. Strong like a lion. But things could break a man."

That was why Ragga had found himself in a maxi heading to Carenage – to find Prince. Like the news said, he was on the beach standing watch over the land he had sketched that no one could name. Ragga didn't know what to say, so he went to buy a cold Guinness in the parlour, hoping to coax the man back to himself. When he returned, no Prince. One minute he was on the beach, the next, gone. The bay, the sea, the road, back home – no Prince. Nobody had seen him any place other than on the beach he'd disappeared from. Like a wave or current had swept him away. All that remained in Ragga's head was the message in the centre of his map.

Panic seized him. He had heard about the Nelson Street arrests. Terence had called to say Keeper was one. He didn't know what to do with the feeling in his bones that Prince wasn't coming back. People could disappear – and that was the reason he went straight to the station.

The police weren't interested.

"Maybe he gone in the bush. You look?"

The wicked smile of the officer behind the counter told him everything. The Gasparee haircutting incident was well known to the police. He was making a big thing out of nothing.

"He leave a message."

The officer grunted and flipped the huge page of his ledger, not bothering to hide his irritation.

"Yes, he write something."

"Where it?"

"You have to come," Ragga replied, already sensing the wall he was about to hit.

"Answer the question: Where is the said message?"

"On the beach... he write it in the sand down by the jetty."

The officer sat back, obviously amused.

"Brother, you here to waste my time?"

"No officer. That is where it is."

"Well, that doh count as evidence."

"But it there, officer, for everybody to see."

"Go home. Curfew going on. Police busy."

The officer resumed his task of copying reports. Unexpectedly, perhaps because of the disappointment on Ragga's face, he sat back again, his hands clasped over his belly, thumbs twirling, as if compelled to maintain an air of nonchalance.

"Look, by law, all you have to do is report a person missing and fill out the form; but police busy, so if he doh turn up by this evening, come back..."

Nothing more to do but head back to the beach; but when he got there, still no Prince. Not even his map. Tide had come in. Most of the little beach had disappeared. Maybe in truth some madness took hold of Ragga when he decided then and there he was going to *The Focus* with his message. People had to know. The least he could do was be the messenger.

"You want to know what I have in that bag?"

He knelt to unzip the knapsack. Leaving the shelter of the porch, Amber followed, feeling the first cool raindrops on her bare arms until the warmth of her own body took over.

With an effortless heave he flipped its contents onto the ground.

"Sand!" she exclaimed.

With one sweep of his hand he flattened the mound.

"Prince write his message here."

He looked up at her steadily with a seriousness that quelled the doubts that stirred in her. The next thing he was standing up on a beach right there in the Beetham.

"Come," he said, extending his hand in welcome.

She hesitated, watching Ragga, his smile like daylight in the dark.

"Doh 'fraid. It have plenty room."

Somebody was taking the weights off her feet and she heard her father's familiar tease: *Girl, life not for spectators.* So she moved forward and took her place.

"When this madness over, I going to set up my own business. All I need is a little place."

"Oh yes, what is that?" Amber asked.

"Electronics, wacker and lawn-mower engines. You name it. I could fix anything. That is my gift," he boasted and pointed heavenwards.

They both fell silent, allowing the hope he had spoken its chance to breathe.

"What about you?"

The question had caught her off guard.

"Me?"

"Yes, you. You like that work you doing?"

"It's a start," she said flatly.

"So where is the finish line?"

The metaphor caught on and they locked eyes.

"We'll see." It was a good time to switch topics. "What was the message – in the sand?"

"New Land. That is what he write."

Wonder illuminated her face.

"New land," she repeated, savouring the words.

And the two of them stood there in the miracle of the revelation, laughing and holding onto each other so they wouldn't ever fall off that island.

TO FIND A WAY BACK

Calvin checked his watch. Siparia was less than an hour away, without interruptions. The problem of the weedlike substance allegedly found at a high official's residence had to be dealt with. His job at the station was to make sure "things" were in order and then get out. A sticky situation – the "evidence" was still there – but he suspected it was all political mischief. It was laughable really, but the possibility that there was truth in the accusation left a sour taste in his mouth. People expected more from those driving the bus. He had no quarrel with that, he was just tired of doing the clean up. Things could go crazy in the blink of an eye. People talked or played both sides. He was anxious to put the whole affair behind him.

The High Street route was at Neil's insistence.

"I hungry, and is deep south we going."

Neil was new to the detective side of policing. They had been working together for just over two years. The "Super" had asked him to show Neil the ropes. Calvin asked no questions, but made sure he kept things above board in all their dealings. He knew how to shut Neil out when necessary, though that required some skilful management.

"The place will be closed like everywhere else."

"I feel like eating dead tonight," Neil persisted. "Jus' swing by."

The youth had a demanding temperament that bothered Calvin. He was more of a bully than zealous. Calvin could smell his hunger. He knew Neil was after something, but he wasn't interested in blocking or protecting any turf, so he played a game of skilful compromise. That was how they ended up on High Street and ran into the drunkard who, Calvin guessed, was Amber's estranged father. The episode shook him but he didn't want Neil to pick up anything.

It was going to be a rough night. Earlier there was the shocker that came over the station's radio about the Minister's collapse and the shooting at Westmoorings. Then there was the Super's last text. Two words: CLEAN UP. The choice of case had offended him. They met only as a last resort. That suited them both. Meetings were uncomfortable. They had entered the Force together. At five years Calvin's senior, the Super had played the role of big brother during their training years. Things had gotten complicated as they moved up the ranks. Now it was easier to avoid face-to-face encounters and be reminded of how far they had strayed from the motto *To Protect and Serve*. Calvin took comfort in that fact that it would soon be over for him. His retirement papers were in. He had made the required years of service and he wanted out.

He decided on the S.S. Erin route, not feeling anymore the need to rush. Even minus the usual traffic, negotiating the tight turnpike to that road always demanded an extra dose of concentration. He pushed aside the feeling of offence the construction represented. More than a visible rip-off, it was, he thought, a blatant insult to people's expectations. Money down the drain – the usual cry.

Once on their way, he relaxed into the drive, content to speed past the growing commercial cluster at Duncan Village. The rain had abated somewhat, so he switched off the air-conditioner and let the window down about halfway. He much preferred the fresh air. Officer Neil snorted. He was fast asleep, his face turned towards the window and his arms folded across his chest. Calvin wasn't surprised. He had worked out Neil's pattern. After confrontations on the job, mostly self-created, he fell into a deep sleep. A coping mechanism, he surmised. Neil was an angry man. He glanced again at him, recalling Amber's accusation.

"The problem with you Mr. Calvin..." – she always addressed him that way – "you really angry with yuhself for some reason only you could tell."

"Me angry?"

He didn't take her seriously. She had a way of arbitrarily tagging him with emotions and traits. Like his preference for Chinese food made him "boring"; his tendency to slip into silence made him "secretive"; but the one that really intrigued him was that his cough – the penalty for too many years of heavy smoking – made him "recalcitrant". It confirmed his sense that what she loved most was words and the destinations they conjured. So he allowed her the liberty of naming him and though he found it easy to dismiss her assertions, later they often opened up questions in him.

"Me angry? You ever hear me raise my voice?"

She never offered any proof for her claims. Like a light switched on and off, she left things there.

The Charlo episode had made him aware of how little he knew about Amber, apart from her job and where she lived. They had become friends over the course of a year, after a series of what seemed like chance meetings at the same newspaper vendor during her lunch breaks. He was stationed at Head Office and had taken to walks in the city to switch gears from police business. That was how he happened to run into her – she was buying papers and he nuts.

It was clear that she was not a real reader in the classical sense. News, people's stories, was what intrigued her. The way she bought her newspapers with an exaggerated concentration attracted him. It told him more about her than she would ever reveal – that she was actually afraid of the world she so thirsted to know. So, after he had broken the ice with some foolishness, he started telling her bits and pieces about his most challenging cases. He soon discovered they shared a common ground that accommodated their friendship – a reluctance to talk about themselves. And although he talked only in a vague way about work, and as fair exchange never asked about her people, he had picked up names and the relationships they matched, mostly through her phone conversations. He was good at piecing stories together. It was his job.

As he approached Palmiste, the remnant trinity of palms silhouetted against the soft wash of the night sky came into view. The rest of their colony had died from some mysterious disease. Pretty soon all from the first planting would be gone. Earlier that year, he had seen a pair of parrots alight on one of the palms. Their sharp cries had pierced him. They had come to mate and nest. He thought it would be a good time to call Amber. He glanced over at Neil – still asleep. There was something he needed to say to her. He readied to call her but hesitated.

Instead, he punched the number-one key and waited. An answering machine kicked in.

"Working," he said at the invitation to leave a message.

Neil coughed and scratched his face. He was growing a beard.

"My radical stylin," he had claimed.

His partner, Calvin sensed, was at the stage when the job was getting complicated. His eyes caught the bulge caused by the service revolver under Neil's windbreaker. He knew the signs, but he didn't want to ask and risk exposing himself so late in the game. It wasn't worth it. Not when his exit was in sight. Neil snored and broke wind.

"Geez, brother!"

Calvin put his window right down and concentrated on guiding the SUV along the winding roads through the abandoned canefields of Phillipine towards Debe. His phone beeped. It was a message from home. One word: *Careful*. He quickly texted back: *Always.* He put the phone facedown on his lap. When he had one of his cleanup jobs, he found it difficult to connect with anyone, particularly Amber. She was the one he preached to about facts. Whilst she had no real background on him, he knew she had done her own puzzling. Maybe that was behind her labels. He had to set things right.

He took a deep breath. The night air carried a hint of burnt cane, a tangy sweetness, as if the now neglected land with its twisted stalks held a past that refused to leave the soil. Something that felt like sadness tightened in his chest and it was with relief that he saw the village appear.

He ignored the red stop light at the intersection where the old railway track ran. The place was strangely deserted. The shops that sold a range of Indian delicacies were closed. He never passed by without stopping for doubles or saheena. The vendors knew him well. They jokingly called him "Boss", and pretended to curry favour by giving him a free doubles or extra channa. Even without a uniform and marked vehicle, they knew his line of work. He played along with their staged deference.

The Erin Road beyond Debe, through Penal and Syne, was not the most comfortable of drives at night, but Calvin enjoyed the poor lighting, the twists and turns of the road, the patches of nothingness mixed in with the small settlements along the way. Once, some years ago, on a solo night trip to Siparia, he had seen a giant snake cross the road at a place he could never name, so there was no way of verifying the occasion.

"Is jumbie or warrau spirit you see. South full ah spirit," the fellas at the station had joked.

"Nah-nah! Is Mami Wata yuh see, and that one mean business, soldier!"

That was Neil's contribution, although the incident had occurred way before his time, but he couldn't help playing Mr Know All. Calvin though knew what he was getting at – what Neil assumed about his relationship with Amber, which he wouldn't otherwise voice. The laughter and picong didn't bother Calvin. He was sure that they all had private jumbies to worry about. Self-defence was awkward business and those who protested loudest usually had cocoa in the sun and were watching for rain.

He knew what he had seen and although he was terrified,

he had come to a complete stop to allow the creature to slither across the road in what seemed like the longest line of a page he had ever followed. When it finally disappeared into the bush, he'd felt that an end was approaching or maybe a different beginning had arrived. He had to simplify his life once and for all. Since that day, he had begun working on writing that new line.

Neil woke again, put down his window, spat, and without missing a beat fell back to sleep. By the time they hit the Penal road, his head was jacked back against the headrest and rolling from side to side with each bend.

The landscape all the way to Siparia was lined with commercial buildings and houses that Calvin knew well, even at night. Some of them looked like structural accidents – whimsically designed and erected by less than expert builders in instalments across the years.

Once he'd been inclined to mock their crude yoking of modern West and old India, the spectacle of their multi-dwelling compartments, massive roofs and ornate columns. One or two had a pavilion-like space on the top floor where family and friends gathered to catch breeze and lime. But slowly he'd come to see it as a world marked by stubborn, even bold efforts to lay down roots and claim visibility on terms that cared little for official approval and standards. They wore their architectural mixing without apology or shame. Now he was almost grateful for their endeavour to shape their way from scratch. He liked to think that he saw in them something of his own dim hope to arrive one day, in spite of the tangles and missteps, in one piece.

Neil woke up suddenly.

"Stop, stop!"

"What is your scene?" Calvin asked irritably.

"I have to take a piss."

He exited the vehicle in a sleep-drunken daze. His cellphone was pinned to his ear as he pissed into a wall of bush.

"Where we reach?" he asked on his return.

"Moora Dam Junction."

"Yuh driving like a tourist, partner," Neil jibed; then stretching out his legs, he folded his arms across his chest and sank into his seat.

The slight was not lost on Calvin, but he chose to ignore it. No sense in complicating things. All this would soon be history. The fella was young in the game and full of himself. He would soon feel the weight he had to carry.

"You will boil down like bhagi. Wait and see," Calvin murmured.

The miles vanished and almost by surprise Siparia's small gathering of neon signs came into view. Calvin remembered his broken promise to drive Amber down to the festival that year. She liked that kind of thing. He wasn't a believer, but he felt drawn to at least swing by the church. The alleged "evidence" lodged at the police station could wait. Mai had powers, people said, and something in him felt broken. So without a glance at the station or courthouse, he headed for La Pastora Street. The fellas were accustomed to his style. He worked on his own time.

The turn-off to La Divina on the hill was upon him when a pick-up seemed to come from nowhere, barging up from the Siparia Old Road.

"What the hell!"

Calvin managed to react in time to avoid a collision. The other driver seemed unaware of the accident he had almost caused. He continued on his way, leaving a cloud of exhaust fumes in his wake, the name PRINCE branded on the tail door. Calvin glanced over at his partner. Still asleep. The man was breaking the law. The pick-up sped along and he found himself following.

The weed business could wait.

Fact plus fact equals truth – the creed that had somehow escaped from him. Had Amber really figured him out, but let him play the mas', the J'ouvert blue devil he took to the streets every Carnival? Had he surrendered behind the blue paint to all that weighed on him and got heavier every year – a life that was now living him? Blue Devil Calvin. The whistle and the biscuit pan sounded louder than the devil of a life that was riding him. He wanted to say to that imposter, "I in charge today. I making my way back, I getting back to that place."

Neil grunted and champed his jaws. Calvin held his breath, not wanting to do anything that might wake him. He would explain the detour later. The SUV sailed along. He took off the strobe lights and allowed enough distance between the vehicles to allay suspicion in the driver ahead. He wanted him to feel he was home free. After Siparia proper, the road to Erin was like an avenue in the bush. It always amazed him. The headlights would pick up rows of fragile dwellings built on slim stilts above the strip of swampland. Each kept touch with the new road by a rickety bridge, though one or two had upgraded to concrete walkways, remnants nevertheless of a past he had often wondered about but never ventured to explore.

PRINCE kept going. Neil remained undisturbed. Rancho Quemado junction appeared. The pick-up made a sharp left turn onto Los Iros Beach Road. Calvin stopped long enough for it to make further headway before he too swung off the Erin Road. His curiosity was piqued. What could the driver be up to? He could see the red taillights growing smaller in the distance. The road led straight to the sea, so there was no fear of losing him. He would wake Neil if needed. A story was ahead of him and he wanted to get to the bottom of it. In fact, he felt that he was being led to meet it.

SCHOLAR'S MARCH

As soon as Matron Wilson saw the man security guards had dropped on her steps like a bundle of wet clothes, she sighed and anchored herself in front of the entrance, arms akimbo.

"Mr. Scholar, is you? What bring you up this side?"

Against his inclination to stand, Scholar sat where he'd been deposited at the bottom of the steps. He was all out of fight. The incident had hit him hard. He had to reconsider his tactics.

"What trouble you get in this time?"

The strain of tenderness in her voice nullified the surface play at a reprimand. She looked towards the guards and then at Scholar.

He hung his head, aware that the men who had detained him hovered but a stone's throw away. No, he wasn't going to fight them again.

"Nurse," one of the men spoke up. "This man shouldn't be on the streets. Do something with him. We have to go back to work."

Matron ignored his interjection.

"What they do you out there?"

A look of the vanquished intimated to her that, in his opinion, he was the one set upon. Matron knew the game. The man had more sense than they granted him. She was certain of that.

"So we not talking today?" she coaxed.

The question was more to establish, for the sake of the guards, where her priorities lay. Whatever their frustrations, they would have to wait.

"Well, you in my yard now, so relax yourself while I deal with these disgruntled fellows."

Scholar was familiar with her professional demeanour – a cultivated blend of proprietorial poise and wary detachment that could not wholly contain either her empathy or her humour. He welcomed the opportunity to recline on the step to take in the action.

She turned her attention to the guards.

"Now tell me, why you bring the gentleman here at this hour?"

"Nurse, the man mad like hell. He cause one big ruction in town. Is better we bring him here than let Besson Street station deal with him."

The request was not procedure, but Matron let it ride.

"I may very well have to relieve you of the gentleman. He is clearly beyond your means to contain; but I would have you know that he wouldn't hurt a fly."

Yes, there was no need to agitate himself. He and Matron Wilson went back a long way. She had his back. They were always on amicable terms. A gift of care, that was what she had. Better than the doctors, who were always quick to inject. She understood his case. There was an informal understanding between them. She respected his mission and he, whenever he was obliged to visit, let her do her job without resistance. So he knew better than to get involved.

"He disrupt the whole of town, and the country under emergency."

An accusing finger pointed at Scholar.

"We can't handle him."

"And that, sirs, we have already established!" Matron concluded.

Without another word, they exited like men making an escape. Matron sighed again and focused on her charge.

"Scholar, what we going to do with you, boy? It's been a long time since you last visited. You were doing so well. Who make you vex? Come, tell me."

Her voice soothed him. She always heard him out without interruption.

"Matron, I will not trouble this esteemed institution further. What transpired at the premises, here unnamed, was the result of a gross misunderstanding. I only blame the inexperience of the young officers at the establishment where I ventured in good faith to do nothing but share my message. I deeply apologise for this untimely intrusion. This unfortunate outcome was not at all what I had hoped for. I am aware you are a very busy woman. I, too, know the importance of time."

He rose awkwardly, using the steps for leverage to push up to his feet.

"Man, where yuh going with all that belly?" Matron asked, switching to the friendly banter that always grounded him. "You look like you ready to drop the child."

Scholar regarded his ample carriage and grinned broadly.

"The quality of your perception is without comparison, Matron. You may in fact be right."

He proceeded to straighten his dishevelled attire.

"Do forgive my appearance. It is the result of an ordeal I would not want to revisit. You know well the standards I keep."

She patiently waited out the fastening of the shirt with the few buttons that were left – regrettably not enough to cover his exposed middle; the securing of the cord that served as a belt; the painful work of fixing the tie and next the finger-combing of his limp mop of hair.

When he was done and stood at attention like a soldier awaiting inspection, Matron judiciously looked him over from her station.

"You could still turn a few heads, Mr Scholar. Now come out of that rain."

Her invitation went unheeded, but she let him be and returned to her duties, leaving him to do what he wanted – to stand exactly on that spot.

Night had fallen when she returned.

"Ok Scholar, penance over," she said jokingly. "Come in and eat something."

From below the shout came, "Ten-shun!"

After delivering a firm military salute, Scholar made a dramatic about-turn and marched off. Matron always took him back to his cadet days.

That marked the end of the routine.

"Walk good," she shouted after him and watched until he disappeared through the gateway.

Scholar was good at walking. But where to go? The lights of the approaching cars hurt his eyes. It had been some time since he had faced the streets at night. To make matters worse, he was without the facility of his loaded cart. He was rarely without it, and he needed to think. Inhaling deeply, he began the trek down the valley. The air, still sweet with wet and the scent of trees, fortified him. Walking, yes, he could do that well. He could walk from San Fernando to Port of Spain, if he had a cause. He could make the whole savannah a hundred times, once he had the mind. And that night, he had one – a conclusion that had suddenly become clearer in the confinement of the van. He had those officers to thank, and that young lady at *The Focus*. The whole misadventure was not in vain.

His destination was Port of Spain, the Square. There was a system to change. The outline of a speech formed as he walked, each step the crystallization of a word he had long been searching for. All the words he had spoken through the years had been seeking one arrival. One conclusion. How could he have missed it? How could he not have spoken it to the public he sought to serve? It was so simple it was almost unbelievable. Who would accept it? The clues were there all along, beneath the theories and the models and the books. But no one had said it. So utterly simple. Or maybe the truth was that it wasn't all that easy. So why bring it up? His style would have to be different. The form of his presentations would have to change. The Square – he had to get there. It was the only place for a revolution.

"A speech like no other, comrades!"

"Okay, soldier, but get out the people road before police put yuh tail in jail."

The speaker was unfamiliar and although the tone was much too impatient, Scholar appreciated the acknowledgement and offered a salute. He would walk all night if he had to. That is what he felt – a need to traverse the entire island, to mark his belonging to every last inch of the place that had given him a word and said, "*Bring it!*"

The message was urgent. His bones told him. The only problem was that without the accompaniment of his cart, he had difficulty deciding what to do with his hands. There was no bar to hold him steady, no music of the moving wheels to carry him. The reassuring weight of all he possessed was not there. His archive of speeches, the library of books he had gathered over the years (though he was vaguely aware one was missing), the wide assortment of pencils and pens he made a habit of collecting, the dismantled cardboard boxes that served him well as writing paper.

His condition hit him.

"Unaccommodated!" he exclaimed, throwing his arms to the sky.

Horns blasted.

"Dads, come out the road! Yuh feel yuh good to eat?"

Something was amiss. He had never experienced such disrespect, not in all his years as a pedestrian in the city. The country was definitely in a mess. The only solution was to press on. He intensified his march, drew his spine long, opened his chest and vigorously swung his arms in time with his feet. That seemed to work. He found a momentum that buoyed him. His destination was the Square. His feet would decide the route. That was the rallying point. The loudspeakers, the crowd of listeners – he would be the one to call the place to attention.

Scholar didn't know the exact moment it happened. Both arms, with their clenched fists, were raised skyward. The feeling was exhilarating. He kept them in the air as he marched on, not stopping for anything, though he could hear the horns honking and people shouting, "Walk on the side." The Square. No relenting until he got there. Then the singing began and he was sure he could walk the whole island... *We shall overcome... we shall overcome one day...*

"Power to that," someone returned at him.

"Yeah man!" he responded.

And jus-so people started to join him, or maybe he fell in with them. Everything, time itself, was seamless. Nothing mattered but that he was moving. Not even the sudden darkness. Blackout. It didn't matter; they were walking together. He wasn't an outsider. Nobody called him, "Indian". No he was "comrade", even back then that April when he was in the middle of that river of bodies heading to the Square. Some fellas fell in with flags and steel drums strung around their necks... People like peas. Yes, this was it. They were making a statement, walking from wherever was their beginning. And he was free to bring with him his side of the story in the place that belonged to everybody. Time to make a change. *We shall overcome... we shall overcome.* That was it. The power of the streets and people wanting change – there was nothing like that flow.

Next thing he knew, she was marching with him, joined in from wherever she came, and they were on the same side. He felt it again, in him, a heart that was bigger than even the "*Power! Power! Power!*" they shouted, and "*Ah never get weary yet...*" that they sang together. A new space was opening. People were marching for something bigger than skin or any God they worshipped – something bigger than whatever was familiar was the real beginning they had made. The answer was already there, always with them. What had gone wrong? Scholar knew one thing: he had to get to the Square.

"Get out the blasted road, ole' timer!" someone shouted.

The man was obviously not a convert, but it didn't matter. He pressed on. A river was flowing. Steel pan and drums, and iron were beating. He was sure he heard a tassa drum rolling. And she was there marching beside him, holding his hand in the ranks.

In all that noise, he asked, "What is your name?"

"Alisha," she said.

Not even from here. Look at that. Just found herself on the island with a dream to live. No passport either. Now, what is that? April – their beginning. He didn't care. Their blood took and both their fists were in the air for a future.

That is the problem with you, Iggy. Too much damn brains and too damn fas'. What yuh doing in creole people business? "Who said that? Who?" He felt the fight in him again. *No-no-no to everything but this island. Even Reverend's scholarship.* "Canada could stay there and freeze. I not in that!" *Throw away everything. And for what? A dry-tail girl from somewhere up the islands? Blasted fool!* "And who the hell say that?" Scholar spun and spun like a dog trying to catch its tail. The crowd was too thick.

"Hold the lady hand, Scholar," a voice directed.

But Alisha was there again in the march to Port of Spain. Her fist in the air. Her Afro like a moon. The solution was clear. Now he had to complete the thing. He had a word to bring, but he needed an assistant when he got to the Square, maybe two. He needed to pass on what he had begun. A simple message.

The march was now a huge river destined to flood the city. People from all over were there: stevedores, sugar-workers, artists, students, taxi-drivers, calypsonians, nurses, coconut vendors, store attendants, office clerks of all kinds, city-council workers, teachers, trade unionists, a few renegade French Creoles, market vendors, journalists, steelband men, party members from all sides – people brave enough to stand in the open and say it was time for a new day. The march was on. He was there. The flow was not his own. He was heading to town.

"O God, Scholar, is you? Come out the people road!"

At least that one knew him. Recognition. Community.

He was on the right track. *Power!* So the chorus went on... *Ah never get weary yet... Ah never get weary yet...* The singing and the march kept him resolute. Never mind the rain and the dark. Alisha too was there and hope burned in him.

Scholar walked all night without incident, apart from a few unkind comments, but he reasoned, *That is life*. People had a right to their opinion. Woodford Square. He never knew how he got there, what route he took or how long he walked to get there. But when he finally stopped and turned around, disappointment loomed. Apart from the sister who followed his every move like a duckling, most, if not all of his comrades had deserted the march. Maybe they had gotten weary and dropped out. Even Alisha – gone. The pursuit of *whys* was futile. The only solution was to carry on. Preach in and out of season. Preach to the empty chairs. Somewhere there was an audience, listening for a word. He moved slowly around the park as one would a home, taking stock, looking for a way to begin. His eyes fell on one faithful soldier fast asleep on a bench not far from his usual speaking spot.

"Young man," he said, tapping his shoulder.

Ivan awoke, more than a little startled. He stared at the man whose face was so much his – though the dishevelled beard covered much of it. He didn't need to ask a question.

"Might I enlist your assistance?"

Scholar directed him to stand in a well-lighted spot. After a quick trip to the bandstand, with the lady in his wake, he returned with three pieces of cardboard, then gathering a handful of mud from the Square's waterlogged ground, he wrote LOVE PEOPLE.

"Here, you hold that, young man."

On the second piece, he formed the word POWER and put it in Ganga's hand.

She stood in line, pleased as punch, holding the word she had learnt on the road.

No more talk. Scholar took his place beside his recruits

with a big smile on his face, ready to give his word: "NEW LAND."

Ivan stood in his place, dazed by the unexpected miracle of the encounter and wondering what he was going to do with the father he had finally found.

LOS IROS

"Come forward, brother. I not blind and I not deaf."

The man sat motionless, a safe distance from the ebb and flow of the tide. His gaze was fixed on the ocean that, under an overcast sky, seemed to Calvin a vast churning void. Was he right to leave Neil asleep in the vehicle? The man had obviously been aware of his presence all along, but it had seemed foolish to even consider that he was being drawn in. Why would he? Their paths had crossed accidently. Calvin took a quick glance back at the distance he had covered. There was no turning back. Cautiously, he moved from the shadows.

"You out late, soldier. Curfew in effect since nine," Calvin said, eyeing the stranger as he inched closer.

The man offered no answer.

An insistent wind drove in off the ocean, letting no leaf rest. A thick carpet of sargassum had invaded the entire beach. Calvin felt the need to anchor his feet.

"Everywhere, weed," he thought, a little amused, remembering the reason he had driven all the way to Siparia.

The wind bore an extra chill on account of the rain that day. Calvin zipped up his windbreaker and thrust his hands into his pockets. He connected with the cold steel of his service revolver. He had almost forgotten it was there. The idea of wearing a holster never sat well with him – the formality of it – like the uniform he'd been happy to discard when he joined the Special Branch Division. Neil thought it sloppy.

"Go ahead, one day you will shoot yuhself."

He was probably right, but he seldom carried a gun, and

when he did, reaching for it was always a last resort. His job required different talents. The SoE, though, had changed the temper of things, a massive *gran charge* of force to beat crime. He wasn't going to be the one to measure the outcome. His own situation was an ole mas on its own. Time to get out. He was more than entitled to go. Take a holiday with the family. There was the safety equipment business he wanted to get going. That talk with Amber was long overdue.

"Tomorrow," he told himself. "Tomorrow. A fresh start."

The driver of the pick-up adjusted his legs. Calvin could hear his long, deliberate intake of air. It had been pure naivety to think he would not be aware that he was being followed. No one else was on the road, and the long stretch to the beach was practically a dark tunnel until the little cluster of lights at the end that opened onto the sea. The pick-up, visibly far from roadworthy, was parked next to the wall of the establishment branded *Beach Boys.* The owners had not anticipated that over the years the intrusion of the sea would authenticate its name.

"I not in nothing, yuh know," the man coaxed, sensing Calvin's caution.

Calvin stood motionless for a while, just behind the man's line of vision. The beach was empty. Nothing seemed amiss. No rendezvous. Nothing underhand. The man seemed more intent on offering his face to the steady drive of the wind that whipped off the sea.

"Look, I holding nothing but this Guinness," he continued, and lifted both hands above his head. One held a black bottle.

Calvin moved closer. The spot were the man sat had been cleared of weeds so it seemed he was cradled in a nest, or was sitting *in* as opposed to *on* the beach.

"It late." Calvin paused, waiting for a reaction. "What is your business here?"

Calvin was now standing with his back to the sea, not directly in front of the stranger, but at an angle that allowed him to see his face and be watchful for any sudden moves.

"Vincent is the name. Vincent Augustine Paul Jacobs. Don't question me about the order. My mother, bless her, took her saints seriously. But you could call me Prince. That is how most people know me."

The wind tore into Calvin's back so that he felt at any moment he would topple over or else be stripped of his clothes. Prince saw his discomfort.

"Brother, I know you represent the law, but the best way to enjoy this beach is to sit down. Take the load off your feet. Like I said, all I holding is this."

He raised the bottle again.

Calvin knew enough to surmise that he really wasn't up to anything. The problem was the seaweed. He didn't relish sitting on it, although the wind took care of the offensive smell.

"Like you could do with some help, a little direction. Here, I clearing a spot."

Prince agilely unfolded his legs and sprang up.

"You hold that. Take a sip if yuh want. This is weather for Guinness."

He chuckled mischievously and began making a clearing on the beach with his bare feet.

"We in business," he said when he was done. "Now take a seat."

Prince crossed his feet and lowered himself back into his place. Calvin returned the drink untouched and sat down, not feeling any need to resist his sense that the stranger was the one in control of the situation. From that angle he saw the sea for the first time, the little erratic waves hustling in. They were like white banners flying in the night sky.

"Sometimes I think, when I watch this sea, the whole sky turn upside down," Prince mused. "Yes, everything is how yuh see."

He sighed and sipped.

"People say I lose my tongue after them fellas cut-off my hair. What they don't know is that I stop talk on my own. So I draw instead. Let them do the talking."

Calvin didn't know what to say. He kept his eyes on the man.

"You from this side?" he eventually asked, mostly to deflect his intuition that he had been directed here to listen.

"No, I from Carenage." He looked towards the sea. "So yuh want to know what I doing down this side? Well, Mr. Officer, I come to Los Iros to find some fresh words to make a start out there." He tipped his head back in the direction of Port of Spain.

Calvin released the tension in his shoulders. He knew exactly what Prince meant; so he found himself listening, forgetting that he was the one with questions to ask the man who was breaking the government's curfew.

"Yes, I come here whenever I run out of living. Behind God back, some people call this place; so I figure if living in front His face so hard, I taking my chances in the back. Let Him take some of the jamming this rounds. Yes, Papa! I needed to take a little rest."

As Prince talked on, Calvin heard himself slowly increasing the depth of his breathing. He had been living from the shallows of his chest like someone waiting for a hammer to fall.

"You know what is the real joke in all this," Prince continued. "Yuh could talk some Spanish? Over there is the Main."

He gestured towards the black horizon and then faced Calvin.

"This island bigger than we think. That is the beauty of this place. And we playing the arse with it. Los Iros – yuh know what that mean?"

Calvin shrugged.

"*The Rocks*. Take that!"

He broke into laughter at the irony he had mapped.

"No getting away! Stand yuh ground until you know different."

Prince offered Calvin another chance at a sip. He decided not to refuse. The man was harmless. Just looking for some relief – a little respite. He understood that feeling.

"I need my strength to go back townside. I need a new page. So I come here to wait."

His posture was relaxed but alert, not so much gazing into the night as giving it permission to envelop him. A smile formed on his lips.

"All this south is a historic place, yuh know."

Prince opened his arms to their full extent. The image fascinated Calvin. There were words for what he looked like. He had heard them somewhere. Maybe something Amber had said; they were lost to him but were there all the same.

"It all started out there – in that channel."

Prince pointed towards the darkened horizon.

"A seated crucifix," Calvin whispered. The image had come back to him, but his words were lost on Prince.

"Imagine that! The whole business we in today, and where we reach up to now, started on that stretch of sea. We can't forget that."

They looked towards the ocean. Beyond the forty or so feet of visibility that the night allowed there was nothing but a boundless rumble.

"The beginning," Prince said and gathered some sand in his hands. "And I don't mean to say that Christo alone responsible for every loss or gain we make. I not saying that. He know me good-good. I have no beef with him. No, sir."

Calvin tried to follow.

"I say, Christo boy, I know what it is to feel you have to prove yuhself to people. Officer, that was the first mistake the fella make. He never really had a firm hold of himself. If yuh ask me, I would say, he was on a runaway when he ended up here. But that is a hunch. Anyway, he get tie-up like market crab trying to please and impress, and he make a royal mess of things. And well, we know what followed."

The wind had picked up its tempo, but there was no sign that it would rain.

"I want to believe he didn't really have no extra dose of bad-mind, not more than anybody else. He wanted to play hero for his people back home, as though that could give him back the *self* he never believed was his own in the first place – or the self he was trying to save by turning explorer. Some bigwig had the last word on his life – that is what mash up the man. What else would make him tell a whole set of lies for no other reason than to look good back home? And I not making no excuse for the history he end up making. Oh no. All I saying is that the greed and hate he well contribute to, and cleared the way for others to pass, they have a root…"

Prince drew closer to Calvin to make his point.

"The real disease, brother, is when a people lose sight of who they are. They think is a race, a faith, a flag, a surname, a title, a bank account, a law, even a hurt that make them who they are. A person, even a people, could fall into that trap."

He broke off to gather some sand, letting it sift through his fingers.

"A person could come to believe they alone have any real right to breathe, think thoughts and feel, build worlds, make themselves happy and celebrate they life. When that is the case, they could look at another person and say, you blocking my way, or you not a part of the future I dreaming for myself and family – or whatever tribe they claim. And when they reach that stage, my brother, they could watch at another person and find everything about themselves better and truer. You understand? So with no proper reason, they give the command – *Get rid of him*."

Prince lay back in the sand, seemingly exhausted. Calvin looked towards the Main, suddenly feeling exposed, all his schemes blown wide open, the many lies he'd helped spin so some anonymous big-shot could walk free or play saint, and he too could have a better life with those damned blue notes. He glanced across at Prince. The empty bottle stood perfectly balanced on his stomach. There was nothing excessive about the man.

"Officer, I come here tonight to remind myself that I want

to write a different story with my life, no matter what face me. This SoE leave me with one memory. They cut off my hair. Well, that is them. I have a story to live, and you see that sky. The first and last letter write up there."

They never heard Neil's approach, but his sharp shout drew them to their feet.

"What going on here?"

His weapon was drawn. Calvin saw the danger. He knew Neil. He used his body to shield Prince.

"Is okay, the fella just come out for some breeze."

Neil wasn't convinced. He stood about twenty feet away cloaked in shadow.

"Show your hands. Let the man show his hands."

Prince stepped in front of Calvin and was about to lift his hands.

"What is that?" Neil shouted, catching sight of the object. "Throw it in the sand."

"Is nothing, Neil. Just stand down."

Calvin could not reason why, but after he had dropped the bottle, Prince decided to turn and run. Maybe he had sensed there was no reasoning that night. Who could tell? He only knew that he had shifted to cover the fleeing Prince, but discovered that Neil had something else in mind. He slumped to the sand like an emptied bag, but felt for the first time in a long time, his heart grow amazingly warm.

THE CATCH

Whole night Aura kept vigil, her thoughts making mayhem in her head. No word. These days anything could happen. People disappearing or getting shoot down. Plenty questions but no answers, as though to know the truth about anything was too much trouble. Better to turn a blind eye and go about your business.

Whole night the dogs moaned and barked in the yard. Nothing. She had fixed her mind on putting on her clothes and going to look for Lucky as soon as curfew lifted in the morning. But where to go – quite up the coast or to the police station down the road? She just didn't know.

Five o'clock sharp, Guts was on the phone saying to stay put, he on his way. That was all. Maybe Lucky was with him. Maybe something happened to the van and he had to stay the night by him. Why he didn't call? Maybe the police had him. But for what? He wasn't in any mischief. Nothing to do but wait.

"Craig is no tief."

That was how Guts started his story, sitting on the edge of the couch like if he wasn't sure he was welcome. Whatever it was, Aura could see the man was uneasy. And no matter how he begged, she refused to sit down, preferring to stand close to the door, as though she was waiting for some signal to dash out to find Lucky, wherever he was.

"Criminal? No, I tell the police straight. That is not the man."

"What yuh mean tief? What happen? Guts, talk quick!"

But he couldn't hurry the telling.

"Aura, believe me. I tell the officer plain. The man he talking 'bout coulda never steal my boat. More than that, he never move with gunman!"

"Boat... gunman? Lord, what is this yuh saying? Where Lucky? Police have him?"

Guts swallowed hard and finally looked Aura in the face. Sorrow. That is what she saw there. Sorrow that made her know the depot had never turned its back on him. It was waiting, like she was waiting, for him to decide to live again.

But Guts was going on like a stuck record.

"Aura, I tell yuh the man not making sense. Police doh believe nonsense. So I tell him, talk sense. And I say plain to the lawmen, I know nothing about him stealing no boat. So I have no charge to press."

"Guts, what yuh saying? Yuh talk to him?"

Distress sapped all the strength from her legs, and she dropped herself into the nearest chair. Guts, seeing her pain, found the strength to let go the way *he* wanted to tell his tale. Better to tell it so the sorrow would flow and flow out of her. So he spoke, and Aura, with her head thrown back against the cushion, listened like she was in some kind of trance.

"After two this morning, police in front my gate telling me to get inside the van. Well, I know better than to quarrel with the law. So I went. Is Fats and Lawrence from the station they send for me. The both of them serious like judge, so I have nothing to say, nothing to ask. I thought I would never reach wherever they were taking me and I too 'fraid to even ask. In the end, Port of Spain Headquarters is where they stop. And that is where they had Lucky in the charge room, and he handcuff.

"Police have him, Guts? What yuh saying to me this morning?"

"Aura, Coast Guard find him in *Stallion* somewhere in the Bocas. Imagine that. No engine. No light. Lucky, I say, my boat? What going on, soldier? Nothing. The man only smiling. I say, 'Lucky, tell the officers what happen out there and tell it straight.' He say a fish pull him."

Guts removed the cap from his head.

"Aura, I had to laugh. The man not making sense, but the police waiting for Lucky to talk. What he was doing out there on the sea? I could see he get real rough up but like that didn't matter. He say he innocent. But I see the situation. They bring me so he could talk. And is my boat they find him in. He tell them that I own the boat, so I too end-up in the comess."

"What he do, Guts? I doh believe whatever they say he do," Aura wailed.

Her distress put fire in Guts to speed up the tale.

"Lucky just not making sense, Aura. But how the story go was that he was out in *Stallion*. That true. He only borrow her. That I believe! Well, he say he sleep-away but when he wake up something was on the line, strong as the devil-self, pulling him out to sea. I say, but Craig, is curfew, why yuh take the boat out in the first place? Yuh think he take me on? He had a meeting to keep, he say. Then like something take him, he shout out in the people station, 'That is my fish!' I begin to feel the next stop for him was the madhouse."

"Man, what yuh talking?"

"Anyway, he say all he could do was hold the line. The night so dark he didn't know where he was, only that he was sure he had his fish, and when he finally decided it was his turn to fight, he start to pull and pull. He feel like he pull that line for years, like that fish was on the next side of the ocean. He say he feel like he was trying to take back from that sea all the loss he lose, even what he didn't even know he lose. Like he was pulling line for him and everybody."

Guts had to stop because Aura started to moan and sob. He grabbed the Limacol from off the centre table and soaked down her head. Poor Aura. She could only repeat like a mantra that she had news for Lucky that morning, but she was waiting for him to sell the land and feel like he was something again.

"I shoulda tell him," she moaned. "All now he would be home."

"Tell him what?"

But the Limacol did its work and she grew silent. Guts figured it was best to get to the end of what he had come to say.

"Night dark and rain nonstop so he couldn't see no more than what was in front of him. Well, when line run out and he hear the thud against the side of *Stallion*, he say, 'Yes, I have him now.' Well that was when, out of nowhere, the Guard appear. Searchlight drop on him."

"I shoulda tell him," Aura groaned.

Guts pressed to the end.

"Well, the Guard shine the light and when Lucky see what was on his line he nearly pass out. A man wrap up like a present in one set ah seaweed."

"O Lord, Lord!" Aura shout. "Guts, what is this yuh telling me?"

"That is the story he tell, Aura, but Lucky, I know, didn't kill nobody. Police say I could make a charge because it is my boat he take. But I not in that! Yuh have my word. Police have to investigate, but the man didn't do no crime."

"Investigate?" Aura scoffed. "Yuh know any crime that solve in this place."

"Doh talk so, Aura. They have no case. And on top of all that, news say they find the lawyer-lady that come for the land yesterday dead. Last night, gunman shoot her up inside her own car. Outside her own house. Not only that. But this is another bacchanal. Shoes, you know Shoes? Police tell me hit and run by Sealots."

"O Lord! Lucky what is this I hearing... What is this, boy?"

"Aura, I tell the man to talk plain, but his concern was with the fish he went out last night to meet, and he believe that dead man had a message for him – that the fish leave his best self on the jetty that day. He jus' never see it so before. That was how he tell it."

All Aura could do was hold her head.

"That is how the man talk. He say, 'Guts, I is a fool in tru'! Is Craig I thought I lose... Well, who the hell is Craig? A blasted coward who feel that life beat you if you get a bruise... Well that man dead.' So he talk. 'That fish save me. You hear what I say. Tell Aura.' The funny thing is, Lucky calm-calm. He talking about moving back to the coast. That he had a place waiting on him to meet again. Too long, he say. Too long he living like a dead man. I tell you, Aura, the man not making no sense."

When Guts finished, Aura sighed longer than a mile. Maybe Craig was finding his way back. Maybe he was beginning to see that is life that he had left behind. Her hands instinctively caressed her belly, feeling for the life growing inside.

MERCY

"Mercy."

Was that the word on her lips? No other word could have been spoken had there been time – no more than the beat of a second. You would want it, would sincerely pray for it, had you too felt utterly helpless – the nakedness of an infant.

Was there even time in the horrible calm of an eye's blink to make a case for life – hers, and all those before and after? Was there a moment human enough for a single saving word to stay the death that ripped through the distance to meet her? Maybe she did speak it – a loud or whispered petition – when she saw him in the night, in the rain. Was he one or legion?

In that breath's pause, did she wonder if a person could know, bone-deep, that her time had come, as in a dream, a premonition, a jumbie bird's cry – or the scent of guava? Was it even possible to ask *why*, like a bewildered child? Conversation – was it too much a civility? Maybe her questions were for others, the invisible ones, the planners of terror with names she could name, but they would not let her. That night, he was but their messenger.

In the sure aim of those headlights, she must have seen his face soaked in rain, no longer shadowed by the night. Did she see in his eyes a glow, a small spark of a far-receded innocence? If one word escaped the prison of her terror, would it have been able to open a space so he could hear her, actually see her? Maybe she could have offered her name, not its two abrupt syllables, but her very self. Would that have been ransom enough to save what they both shared, in blood, in human flesh? Might he then have been no longer a loaded gun for her, or anyone?

Questions – the hallmark of her labour – the endless pursuit of answers. Do we want them – the answers that would make the law a friend and almost a saviour? Maybe there will come a day when they will be wanted.

And what was her failure or error? Who is without those texts we write in sand and wait for a wave to offer, like a saviour, a new page? In that split second, in the middle of the road, with the rider facing her, was there in her, in us, a small cry for forgiveness? Would he have heard it, the man in the rain, who had chosen to know her no more than his paid purpose? If one final plea was available to her – anybody – what might that have been? But in that dread facing... could hope blossom?

"Mercy."

Someone said that word was in the wind. It was heard weeping like a thousand mothers for their lost children. Dare we listen? She lived it like a creed that finally took everything she was. *Paradise*, if ever it existed, was her one true labour – to birth, together, a place where mercy *is* home. Not a dream of shelter, a utopia, but the grace of standing, no matter how briefly, on this island, a world, as in a spot of sunlight, healed of every beginning – like an arrival past blame, the dance of a city's street.

And that young man in the rain, carrying death on his back, did she think that someone had failed him? This place? Did anyone care to ask? Maybe she asked it for us, and for the very ones who are now saying: *This string of wonderings, author, is not a story. It tells no tale. Zero marks!* Well, correct is right, as they say. It isn't. And that perhaps was the point of her life – in the end. There are places where stories cannot follow, even though they try to, like stumbling disciples. So now we want a story to let us off the hook – play-ah-mas' for us because we cannot love enough to save what is precious. Was that the real EMERGENCY, ours to claim? Mercy has another face. What is it?

"Unconquerable." So we named her – needing her to be larger than life – for her audacity in not turning a blind eye. Somebody had to punish her for raising the bar too high. More than flesh – that was the mas' we put her in to save ourselves. That was the first bullet. If only she could have spoken, even without a word, maybe something stifled would have been set free in the man who pointed death at her. He might have stayed his hired hand.

Had she the time or the presence of mind to kill her headlights sooner, they – he and she – might have had a second to meet. One second, a heartbeat, could have changed the face of that tragic night. Maybe the shadows hidden behind him, that posse of ten, eleven, twelve, would have, one by one, come into the light. And the thirteenth, the one who would never see a jail, maybe he or she would have put death away, too. Had she asked too much of this place? In a split second, a new kind of meeting – was it possible?

"Mercy."

Girl, let the bobol pass. Someone may have spoken those words to her. Someone who loved her and wanted to remind her what happened in this place when you batted outside your crease. Perhaps it didn't matter. She knew too well the farce, and why the law had been made accomplice. Section Thirty-Four; improprieties in the judiciary; in the office of the DPP; the supermarket kidnapping; the cocaine in juice tins. No chronology mattered. No adequate list. There was one disease.

Yet, *Trinidad is nice…* It might have been that she actually believed it, beyond the necessary irony. That night, especially, she wanted to speak that one word to make *paradise* real, to create one precious moment between herself and the man poised to kill – a chance to return to belief.

"Mercy."

Was it written on her face? Or did she scream behind the tinted glass of that coffin she drove? If, indeed, a howl of terror escaped, was it hers alone? So large an agony could never be so small, so private. Did disbelief dawn? There was no higher law to save her. In that fraction of a second, on that road to home, maybe she saw again the horizon on her island's north coast. Maybe she hoped that we had not forgotten the Scripture of ourselves...

...In the beginning was the struggle and the tears from the maraca to Canboulay. In the beginning was the word of the drum... the pan and the steel, with the tassa not simply blending, with the strings of a violin too... A new beat... In the beginning was this moving towards the oneness we are and celebrate deeper than skin-teeth. Not the washing of hands – never the gloating at some lie of private blessedness. Never this carnage of our lives.

Remember ourselves... Re-member...

There is a time when fiction, too, must end – a time for mourning. All talk done. Hush, now. Hush... Let mercy rain.

ABOUT THE AUTHOR

Jennifer Rahim is a widely published poet, fiction writer and literary critic. She worked for many years as a Senior Lecturer at the University of the West Indies, St. Augustine campus. She attained an MA in Theology from the University of St. Michael's College, Toronto (2016). With Barbara Lalla, she edited and introduced two collections of essays, *Beyond Borders: Cross-Culturalism and the Caribbean Canon* (2009) and *Created in the West Indies: Caribbean Perspectives on V.S. Naipaul* (2011). Her poetry collection *Approaching Sabbaths* (2009) was awarded a prestigious Casa de las Américas Prize in 2010. *Redemption Rain: Poems* was published in 2011 and *Ground Level: Poems* in 2014. *Songster and Other Stories* (2007) is her well-received collection of short stories. *Curfew Chronicles: A Fiction* (2017) is her second collection of stories.

ALSO AVAILABLE

Songster and Other Stories
ISBN: 9781845230487; pp. 145; pub. 2007; price £8.99

Rahim's stories move between the present and the past to make sense of the tensions between image and reality in contemporary Trinidad. The contemporary stories show the traditional, communal world in retreat before the forces of local and global capitalism.

A popular local fisherman is gunned down when he challenges the closure of the beach for a private club catering to white visitors and the new elite; the internet becomes a rare safe place for an AIDS sufferer to articulate her pain; cocaine has become the scourge even of the rural communities. But the stories set thirty years earlier in the narrating 'I's' childhood reveal that the 'old-time' Trinidad was already breaking up. The old pieties about nature symbolised by belief in the presence of the folk-figure of 'Papa Bois' are powerless to prevent the ruthless plunder of the forests; communal stability has already been uprooted by the pulls towards emigration, and any sense that Trinidad was ever edenic is undermined by images of the destructive power of alcohol and the casual presence of paedophilic sexual abuse.

Rahim's Trinidad, is though, as her final story makes clear, the creation of a writer who has chosen to stay, and she is highly conscious that her perspective is very different from those who have taken home away in a suitcase, or who visit once a year. Her Trinidad is 'not a world in my head like a fantasy', but the island that 'lives and moves in the bloodstream'. Her reflection on the nature of small island life is as fierce and perceptive as Jamaica Kincaid's *A Small Place*, but comes from and arrives at a quite opposite place. What Rahim finds in her island is a certain existential insouciance and the capacity of its people, whatever their material circumstance, to commit to life in the knowledge of its bitter-sweetness.

Between the Fence and the Forest
ISBN: 9781900715270; pp. 88; pub. 2007; price £7.99

Adopting the persona of a douen, a mythical being from the Trinidadian forests whose head and feet face in different directions, Jennifer Rahim's poems explore states of uncertainty both as sources of discomfort and of creative possibility.

The poems explore a Trinidad finely balanced between the forces of rapid urbanisation and the constantly encroaching green chaos of tropical bush, whose turbulence regularly threatens a fragile social order, and whose people, as the descendants of slaves and indentured labourers, are acutely resistant to any threat to clip their wings and fence them in.

In her own life, Rahim explores the contrary urges to a neat security and to an unfettered sense of freedom and her attraction to the forest 'where tallness is not the neighbour's fences/ and bigness is not the swollen houses/ that swallow us all'. It is, though, a place where the bushplanter 'seeing me grow branches/ draws out his cutting steel and slashes my feet/ since girls can never become trees'.

Approaching Sabbaths
ISBN: 9781845231156; pp. 132; pub. 2009; price: £8.99

These poems move seamlessly between the inwardly confessional, an acute sensitivity to the distinctive subjectivities of an immediate circle of family, friends and neighbours, and a powerful sense of Trinidadian place and history. Few have written more movingly or perceptively of what can vex the relationship between daughters and mothers, or with such a mixture of compassion and baffled rage about a daughter's relationship to her father. If Sylvia Plath comes to mind, acknowledged in the poem 'Lady Lazarus in the Sun', the comparison does Rahim no disfavours; Rahim's voice and world is entirely her own. There is in her work a near perfect balance between the disciplined craft of the poems, and their capacity to deal with the most traumatic of experiences in a cool, reflective way. Equally, she has the capacity to make of the ordinary something special and memorable.

Here is no self-indulgent misery memoir, not least in its compassion and involvement with other lives. The threat and reality of fragmentation – of psyche's, of lives, of a nation – is ever present, but the shape and order of the poems provide a saving frame of wholeness. Poem after poem offers phrases of a satisfying weight and appositeness, like the description of the killers of a boy as 'mere children,/ but twisted like neglected fields of cane'.

Winner of a Casa de las Américas Prize 2010 – one of Latin America's oldest and most prestigious literary awards. The jury said the collection "captures a sense of the complexities of historical, social and cultural aspects of contemporary Caribbean".

Ground Level
ISBN: 9781845232054; pp. 100; pub. 2014; price: £8.99

In 2011 the Government of Trinidad & Tobago declared a state of emergency to counter the violent crime associated with the drugs trade. *Ground Level* confronts the roots of the madness and chaos seething under the surface of this "crude season of curfew from ourselves" when the state becomes a jail. For Rahim, her country is a place where "No-one hears the measure of shadow in any rhythm", a place where "poets hurt enough to die".

In this dread season, Rahim finds hope and consolation in the word and in those places where it is possible to find salvation in "this landscape of ever-opening doorways", such as Grand Riviere, the subject of a long, twelve-part reflection on the values that can still be found in rural Trinidad. Elsewhere she engages in dialogue with those writers who confronted the Janus face of Caribbean creativity and nihilism:

writers such as Earl Lovelace, Eric Roach, Victor Questel, Derek Walcott, Kamau Brathwaite and Martin Carter, praying of the last "let his words drop on the conscience of a nation". Alluding to the late Jamaican poet Anthony McNeill, she confides that "The Ungod of things has not changed".

This is an ambitious collection that speaks in both a prophetic and a literary, intertextual voice, which combines the personal and the public in mutually enriching ways; it shows the assurance of a poet who has constantly worked at her craft, but who also takes formal risks to capture the reality of desperate times.